READ ALL THE CANDY FAIRIES BOOKS!

Chocolate Dreams
Rainbow Swirl
Caramel Moon
Cool Mint
Magic Hearts
Gooey Goblins
The Sugar Ball
A Valentine's Surprise
Bubble Gum Rescue
Double Dip
Jelly Bean Jumble
The Chocolate Rose
A Royal Wedding
Marshmallow Mystery
Frozen Treats
The Sugar Cup
Sweet Secrets
Taffy Trouble

COMING SOON:

The Coconut Clue
Rock Candy Treasure

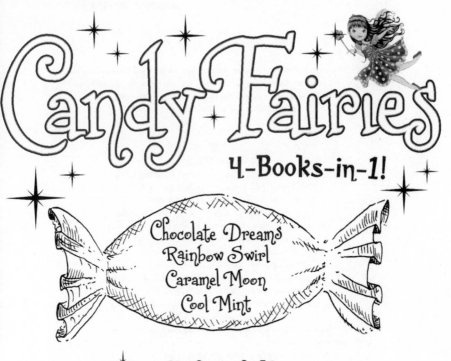

Candy Fairies

4-Books-in-1!

Chocolate Dreams
Rainbow Swirl
Caramel Moon
Cool Mint

HELEN PERELMAN

ILLUSTRATED BY
ERICA-JANE WATERS

ALADDIN
NEW YORK LONDON TORONTO SYDNEY NEW DELHI

ALADDIN

An imprint of Simon & Schuster Children's Publishing Division
1230 Avenue of the Americas, New York, New York 10020
This Aladdin hardcover edition June 2015
Chocolate Dreams text copyright © 2010 by Helen Perelman
Chocolate Dreams illustrations copyright © 2010 by Erica-Jane Waters
Rainbow Swirl text copyright © 2010 by Helen Perelman
Rainbow Swirl illustrations copyright © 2010 by Erica-Jane Waters
Caramel Moon text copyright © 2010 by Helen Perelman
Caramel Moon illustrations copyright © 2010 by Erica-Jane Waters
Cool Mint text copyright © 2010 by Helen Perelman
Cool Mint illustrations copyright © 2010 by Erica-Jane Waters
Cover illustration copyright © 2010 by Erica-Jane Waters
Also available in individual Aladdin hardcover and paperback editions.
All rights reserved, including the right of reproduction in whole or in part in any form.
ALADDIN is a trademark of Simon & Schuster, Inc., and related logo is a
registered trademark of Simon & Schuster, Inc.
For information about special discounts for bulk purchases, please contact
Simon & Schuster Special Sales at 1-866-506-1949 or business@simonandschuster.com.
The Simon & Schuster Speakers Bureau can bring authors to your live event.
For more information or to book an event contact the Simon & Schuster Speakers Bureau at
1-866-248-3049 or visit our website at www.simonspeakers.com.
Cover designed by Neil Swaab
Interior designed by Karina Granda
The text of this book was set in Berthold Baskerville Book.
Manufactured in the United States of America 0515 FFG
2 4 6 8 10 9 7 5 3 1
Library of Congress Control Number 2015938608
ISBN 978-1-4814-6018-7
ISBN 978-1-4169-9869-3 (*Chocolate Dreams* eBook)
ISBN 978-1-4169-9870-9 (*Rainbow Swirl* eBook)
ISBN 978-1-4424-0716-9 (*Caramel Moon* eBook)
ISBN 978-1-4424-0963-7 (*Cool Mint* eBook)
These titles were previously published individually by Aladdin.

Contents

BOOK 1   Chocolate Dreams   1

BOOK 2   Rainbow Swirl   115

BOOK 3   Caramel Moon   225

BOOK 4   Cool Mint   337

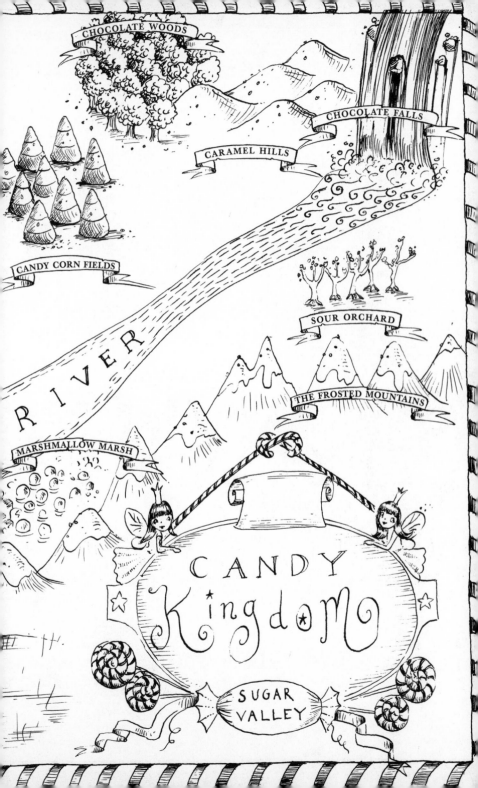

Chocolate Dreams

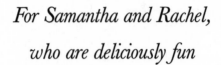

For Samantha and Rachel,

who are deliciously fun

Contents

CHAPTER 1   Sweet Spring   5

CHAPTER 2   A Big Chocolate Surprise   14

CHAPTER 3   A Chocolate Mess   22

CHAPTER 4   A Sour Sight   32

CHAPTER 5   Bittersweet News   42

CHAPTER 6   A Chocolate Promise   51

CHAPTER 7   A Dangerous Plan   59

CHAPTER 8   Black Licorice   69

CHAPTER 9   Chocolate Dreams   79

CHAPTER 10   A Touch of Chocolate   86

CHAPTER 11   Dark Chocolate Wishes   95

CHAPTER 12   Solid Chocolate   104

1

Sweet Spring

Wait for me!" Cocoa the Chocolate Fairy called. She fluttered her wings and flew after her friend.

"Come on," Melli cried over her shoulder. Her caramel-colored dress sparkled in the sunlight. "Let's go!" Her purple wings flapped quickly as she soared ahead.

Cocoa took a deep breath as she caught up to her friend. The smell of chocolate from the roaring Chocolate River made her smile. This was her favorite spot in the entire Candy Kingdom.

Everything looked delicious this bright morning. The morning sun sprinkled light over colorful Sugar Valley. Spring was the most glorious season in the kingdom. All the candy flowers and trees were in bloom, and fairies everywhere were celebrating. A new season of candy had begun!

Cocoa spotted their friends on the sugar banks of the Chocolate River. Raina was easy to see with her bright red wings. And next to her was tiny Dash in her white shimmering dress and her small silver wings.

"There they are!" Cocoa said, pointing. She sailed down close to the river. All the new chocolate flowers were sprouting up along the shoreline. Chocolate wildflowers were always so sweet and colorful!

What a choc-o-rific morning, she thought.

"What took you so long?" Dash asked when she saw her friends. The tiny Mint Fairy might have been one of the smallest fairies in Sugar Valley, but she was also the fastest. And not always the most patient!

Cocoa came to a landing beside her friends. She pointed to the east side of the kingdom, where she and Melli lived. "We had the longest distance to fly," Cocoa said. "Besides, we're not *that* late. Berry isn't even here yet."

"Oh, peppermint sticks!" Dash exclaimed. "Berry's always late."

Berry was a Fruit Fairy who always took her sweet time getting ready. She liked everything perfect, from her hair to her toenails. By far, she was one of the most glamorous fairies in Sugar Valley. But she was a very good friend.

Raina patted a spot next to her on the white sugar sand. "Come, sit down, Cocoa," the Gummy Fairy said kindly. "You must be tired."

All Gummy Fairies had a gentle spirit. Their spirit helped them with the difficult task of watching over Gummy Forest. Growing gummy crops and tending to the gummy animals was hard work. But Raina had proved to have the most patience. She was the Gummy Fairy in charge of the gummy animals in Gummy Forest. Even with the pesky gummy worms and mischievous gummy fish, Raina never lost her cool. But above all, she didn't like messes—or fights with her friends.

"I brought you all something," Melli said cheerfully. She reached into her bag and pulled out caramel sticks. "Fresh caramel!" she exclaimed. She handed one to each of her friends.

"Delicious," Dash exclaimed. She was tiny, but she was always hungry! She loved the thick caramel sticks that grew at the top of Caramel Hills. All Caramel Fairies were able to make caramel, but Dash knew that Melli's sweet touch and generous heart made these caramels the best in the kingdom.

"Thank you!" Cocoa said. "I'm starving. I've been rolling chocolate eggs all morning." She

took a bite of the sweet stalk. "Did you know that each egg has to be turned every hour?" She looked around at her friends.

"We know," Berry said playfully. She couldn't help but gently tease her friend. "To get the eggs the perfect shape, they need to be turned every hour." She grinned. Cocoa had been telling them that for weeks now!

Every spring one Chocolate Fairy was chosen to care for the first spring chocolate eggs. This year Cocoa was that proud fairy.

On the first day of spring Cocoa would deliver the eggs to Candy Castle. Royal Foil Fairies worked all winter to create beautiful foil to decorate the eggs for the Egg Parade.

The parade of chocolates moved through Sugar Valley and was a joyous event. There were floats full of chocolates for all to view. But everyone waited to see the delicate sugar basket filled with the foil-wrapped eggs. The eggs were presented to the fairy princess in the Royal Gardens of Candy Castle. A glorious chocolate feast was held afterward to celebrate. All the fairies looked forward to the festive event.

"It is a big honor to be in charge of the eggs," Melli said. She stood up and walked over to the proud Chocolate Fairy. "And, Cocoa, you are doing a great job."

Cocoa smiled. "Thanks." She stood up with her hands on her hips, and spread her golden wings. "The eggs are getting big already!" she boasted.

"Big enough?" Dash asked. "Bigger than me?"

Her minty nature definitely gave her a cool attitude.

"The eggs need to get bigger," Cocoa replied. "And they will. These are the first spring chocolates." Cocoa fluttered her wings. "This is going to be the best crop of eggs Candy Kingdom has ever seen. You can be sure as sugar that they'll be the biggest and best yet!"

2

A Big Chocolate Surprise

Cocoa leaned back and looked up at the sky. She loved being with her friends—and taking a rest from watching the eggs! She bit another chunk out of her caramel stalk. "After these eggs are delivered to the castle, I'm going to sleep for a whole day!"

"Hey, lazy wings!" Berry called cheerfully from the air. She gracefully landed next to Cocoa on the sugar sand. The beautiful Fruit Fairy smoothed out her raspberry-colored dress. "What are you fairies up to this delicious morning?"

"Waiting for you," Cocoa said, rolling her eyes. "What else is new?"

"What's got your wings all in a tangle?" Berry asked. "I'm right on time."

Raina stood up. "Well, we're all here now," she said kindly. She grinned at her friends. "And that is what's important."

"That's true," Melli said. "Let's have some fun!"

The five fairies ate their caramels and talked about the upcoming Egg Parade.

"I'm going to wear a chocolate-leaf crown," Cocoa declared. "I've already started to look for the best leaves."

"And I'm going to wear a new fruit-chew necklace," Berry said. She dug her hand into her pocket to show the sparkling sugar-coated jewels. "I just picked them yesterday." She held out her hand to show her friends.

"Oh, Berry!" Melli cried. "Those are beautiful. You have the best taste."

"They'll make a really nice necklace," Dash told her. She peered into her friend's hand. "But they certainly look good enough to eat!"

Cocoa laughed. "Berry, you'd better hide those from Dash. You always know how to dress up an outfit with delicious treats."

"A fairy has to know how to accessorize!"

Berry said, grinning. She touched her head. Sparkly sugar clips held her dark, thick hair up in a perfect bun. "There are some great new fashions this spring," she added.

"That's for sure," Raina told her. "Everything about spring is so sweet, isn't it?"

"You say that about every season," Dash kidded her. She flew up to a chocolate flower, plucked it, and dipped her hand into the gooey mint center. "But I have to agree. These spring flowers are very good!"

"Mmm, let me have a taste," Melli said. She flew over to Dash and took a piece of the fresh flower. "You are right," she said, licking her fingers. "These are good."

Raina stood up and faced Gummy Forest. A gentle wind ruffled her red wings. She closed

her eyes. "I have to get back to the forest," she said.

"Will you be at Sun Dip later on?" Melli asked.

Sun Dip was a special time when the sun dipped below the Frosted Mountains, casting a beautiful evening light on the valley. All the fairies in Sugar Valley gathered to feast on their candy crops before they settled in for the night. It was the best part of the day!

"Can't wait!" Cocoa exclaimed, spreading her wings to fly.

"Wouldn't miss it!" Dash shouted.

"Me too," Raina and Berry said at the same time.

Cocoa and Melli took off together for the eastern part of Sugar Valley. They waved good-bye to Berry, Dash, and Raina. Together, they flew back up Chocolate River, over Lollipop Landing, and to Chocolate Woods.

"Don't forget the caramel corn," Cocoa said. "We can dip them in chocolate tonight. I'll bring a bucket from Chocolate Falls. We can make chocolate dip surprises for everyone. It will be fun!"

"Sounds good," Melli answered. "I won't forget."

"Race you!" Cocoa shouted as she soared into Chocolate Woods. She loved a race! Skillfully, she dodged in and around the tall trees and quickly pulled ahead of Melli.

As she flew toward the rumbling of Chocolate Falls, Cocoa's eyes grew wide with fear. Just before Melli had to turn off for Caramel Hills, Cocoa gasped.

"Oh, sweet sugar!" Cocoa cried. She pointed to the chocolate egg nest on top of the tallest chocolate oak tree. The nest was empty! The chocolate eggs were gone!

A Chocolate Mess

Cocoa couldn't believe her eyes. She flew over the empty chocolate nest. Where could the eggs have gone?

Maybe this is just a bad dream, she thought. She blinked her large brown eyes, but the nest was still bare! Her heart pounded in her chest. She shouldn't have left the eggs alone! But she never thought anything would happen to them. . . .

"The eggs!" Melli exclaimed. She touched down on the edge of the nest next to Cocoa. Her purple wings flapped quickly.

Cocoa shook her head. The whole kingdom was counting on her to deliver the chocolate eggs for the Egg Parade. And now she'd let everyone down.

A few weeks ago Fairy Princess Lolli had flown to Chocolate Woods and picked Cocoa to watch over the eggs. Cocoa had felt so special! In front of everyone in Chocolate Woods, she had made a promise to care for the eggs.

Having the royal fairy princess come to her home had been such a special treat. Everyone loved the beautiful fairy princess. Princess Lolli had a heart of sugar and was fair and true. She

cared for all the Candy Fairies and made Sugar Valley the sweetest place to live.

Princess Lolli will be so disappointed! Cocoa thought. She didn't want to upset the fairy princess. Not to mention the Royal Foil Fairies who were hard at work painting the elaborate wrappers for the eggs!

All her chocolate dreams were melting away.

"This is all my fault!" Cocoa cried. "No fairy has ever lost the chocolate eggs."

"Maybe they just rolled out?" Melli said hopefully. Melli always tried to see the bright side, but Cocoa couldn't see one at the moment.

Cocoa flew below the heavy branches of the chocolate oak tree. She knew eggs falling from the nest would be very unlikely. The nest was woven from the strongest chocolate branches.

Each one had been carefully picked. The idea of the eggs slipping or falling out didn't seem possible.

"Melli, they're not here," Cocoa whispered. "The Egg Parade is in two days. I can't create new eggs in time!"

Chocolate Fairies had chocolate magic. They could create chocolate candy with a simple touch. But unlike regular chocolate eggs, the spring eggs needed time to grow. Everyone in the kingdom counted on those eggs being in the Egg Parade. They needed to be extra-special!

"Let's keep looking, then," Melli said. She smiled at her friend. "I'm sure we'll find them."

Cocoa and Melli carefully searched Chocolate Woods. The bushes and trees were bursting with chocolates, and the rich, dark soil smelled delicious. But there were no eggs anywhere . . . not even a clue.

The two fairies flew in and out of the rows of trees looking for any sign of the eggs.

"Let's check under the chocolate chip bushes," Melli told Cocoa. She pointed to the low, prickly bushes around the old chocolate oak tree.

"I guess it is possible that they rolled under there," Cocoa said. She was willing to look anywhere for the precious eggs.

The short twig branches of the chocolate chip bushes tickled Cocoa's wings, but she crawled under several of them anyway.

"Melli, what am I going to do?" Cocoa cried. Tears were in her eyes. She sat at the bottom of the old chocolate oak. Her wings rubbed against the rough chocolate bark. "Everyone was counting

on me! How could this have happened?"

"It's not your fault," Melli told her. "Come, quick." She pulled Cocoa's hand. "Let's cover the nest before anyone sees." She put her hand on Cocoa's shoulder. "That will give us time to figure something out."

Together, the two fairies pulled three large chocolate leaves over the nest. As they covered the nest, Cocoa thought about her morning. She had checked on the eggs and rolled them. The morning was no different from any other in the past few weeks. This was a real mystery. Or was it?

When the nest was covered, Cocoa looked up at her friend. "Melli," she said softly, "do you think someone *stole* the eggs?"

As a young fairy, Cocoa had heard stories

about candy stealing. But those were just fairy tales. She had never heard of chocolate eggs being stolen from their nest! And so close to the Egg Parade!

"Stolen?" Melli gasped. She had also heard the stories, but she thought that's all they were—stories. "You don't really believe all those fairy stories, do you?"

"But how else do we explain this?" Cocoa exclaimed.

"I suppose someone *could* have stolen the eggs," Melli said. She thought about that idea for a moment. "But who would steal the spring eggs?" she wondered out loud. "Who would do such a sour thing?"

Cocoa shuddered. She immediately knew the answer to Melli's question. There was only one creature sour enough in Sugar Valley. Her wings twitched. She didn't want to say what she was thinking.

"We're going to need more help," Melli said. She fluttered her wings nervously. "Raina, Berry, and Dash will know what to do. I'll send word for them to meet us here."

As Melli sent a sugar fly to deliver the messages, Cocoa sat with her head hanging low. She wanted to believe that her friends could help her. But this was a huge problem. This was one huge chocolate mess.

More than anything, Cocoa wanted to make this situation right. She'd need every ounce of chocolate courage she had. She hoped her friends would get there soon.

4

A Sour Sight

Raina was worried. The message from Melli didn't make sense to her. How could the chocolate eggs be missing? The sugar fly that delivered the message had also told her to find Berry and fly as fast as they could to Chocolate Woods. Sugar flies only delivered short messages, so she'd have to wait until she saw Cocoa to get the whole story.

As fast as she could, Raina flew to Lollipop Landing. She spotted Berry right away, putting the finishing touches on her cherry lollipops.

"Berry!" Raina called. She flew up to her and grabbed her arm.

Berry was surprised to see her friend. But as soon as she saw her, Berry knew something was wrong. Raina's worried expression and her shivering wings made Berry concerned. When Raina told her what had happened, Berry left her lollipops and they flew off to Chocolate Woods.

Cocoa needed them. And the two Candy Fairies were on their way.

"I don't understand," Berry said. She was soaring through the air as fast as she could. "Chocolate eggs *don't* disappear."

"No, they don't," Raina said, agreeing. "All of Candy Kingdom is waiting for those eggs—and the Egg Parade! Spring isn't official until those eggs are delivered!"

"The sugar fly didn't say anything else?" Berry asked. She knew that Raina often overreacted. But in this case, she understood. Missing chocolate eggs were something to be very concerned about.

"No, he had no other information," Raina said. "The fly just delivered the message and then flew off. He was off to Peppermint Grove to find Dash next."

Raina took a deep breath. *This isn't good news,* she said to herself. She thought of her friend, and shook her head. "Poor Cocoa!" she cried.

The two fairies flew up along Chocolate

River to Chocolate Woods. Raina glanced down at the roaring river. She put her hand up to her eyes to shield the glare from the sun. Was she imagining things? She shook her head and then looked down below again. She slowed her wings and pointed to the river.

"Berry!" she cried in a hushed whisper. "Look!"

Following Raina's finger, Berry looked down below. She squinted her blue eyes as she watched the scene.

"Come on! Let's get closer!" Berry said. She quickly dove down to get a better look at the river. As she flew closer, she saw what had caught Raina's eye. Hiding behind a large wild fruit-chew bush, she and Raina watched carefully. Furry little Chuchies were crossing the river. They were carrying a black licorice stretcher filled with Cocoa's chocolate eggs!

The Chuchies lived in the salty pretzel stalks near Black Licorice Swamp. Although they lived in the swamp, they loved fairy candy. The Chuchies were sneaky creatures who would do anything to get it!

Raina peered over Berry's shoulder in disbelief. "I've never seen the Chuchies in Candy Kingdom!" she whispered.

"Mogu!" Berry whispered to her. She narrowed her eyes. This bitterness could only come from one Sugar Valley creature. Just thinking of him made her scowl.

Raina gasped. Hearing that name sent a chill down to the tips of her wings. Mogu was a salty old troll who lived under the bridge in Black

Licorice Swamp. His sour nature was part of what made the swamp bitter and dark.

"You know that the Chuchies do whatever Mogu asks because he gives them candy," Berry said.

"*Stolen* candy," Raina said.

The old troll usually kept to himself and stayed under his bridge. But he was known to have candy cravings. . . .

But would he stoop to stealing? Raina wondered.

"Those furry little thieves never act alone," Berry said. She squinted her eyes as she watched. "They do whatever old Mogu tells them to do. He must be behind this!"

This situation was worse than Raina could have imagined. Nowhere in the Fairy Code Book was there any information about getting chocolate eggs back from Black Licorice Swamp! She watched as the Chuchies waddled across the river. There was nothing the two fairies could do. Candy Fairies had limited power across the river.

This was a very sour situation!

"What are we going to do?" Raina cried. Her wings started to twitch nervously.

"First, you have to calm down," Berry instructed. She looked Raina in the eye. "We have to tell Cocoa." Then she turned to watch the Chuchies cross the river. "Those rotten little thieves," she grumbled. "How dare they steal fairy chocolate!"

"But, Berry," Raina pleaded, "if you tell Cocoa that we saw the Chuchies with the eggs, she'll want to go see Mogu herself!" She shook her head, making her long hair fly in the breeze. "She's crazy enough to make that journey across the river and over the Frosted Mountains. We can't let her do that!"

Berry nodded her head, agreeing. "It would be just like Cocoa," she said. "But we have to tell her the truth. Someone needs to save the eggs. Now that the Chuchies took them across the river, we have to do something. Fast."

"I was afraid you were going to say that," Raina said.

5

Bittersweet News

Raina and Berry found Cocoa and Melli sitting at the bottom of the old chocolate oak tree.

"This is the gooiest mess of all time," Cocoa said. When she saw her friends coming, she looked up at them. Seeing them gave her a little bit of hope. She was glad her friends were there. "What am I going to do?" she cried.

"Mogu has the eggs," Berry told her before her feet even touched the ground. Berry always told things straight, and this news was too big to sugarcoat.

"Mogu!" Cocoa exclaimed. "That salty old troll! I knew it!"

Melli's mouth dropped open. "What?!"

"We saw the eggs," Berry went on. She moved closer to Cocoa. "They are safe," she said. Then she added, "For now."

"Holy peppermint!" Dash cried as she swooped into the Chocolate Woods. She was a bundle of excited energy. "Was that sugar fly for real? Are the eggs really gone?"

"Shhh," Melli scolded. She reached up and grabbed Dash's tiny hand. "We don't need every fairy in the kingdom to hear." She turned back to

Berry. "What are you talking about? Where did you see the eggs?"

Berry watched the look on each of her friends' faces. She was used to fairies gawking at her. Fairies usually stopped her to admire her beautiful wings or clothes, but this was different. This was serious. "Raina and I saw the Chuchies carrying the eggs over Chocolate River. They had a stretcher made out of black licorice."

Melli, Dash, and Cocoa gasped.

"Are you sure?" Melli asked Raina and Berry.

Raina quickly nodded her head. "They were Chuchies, all right. And they must have been following Mogu's orders, as usual." She rushed over to Cocoa. "Oh, Cocoa!" she cried. "I am so sorry!"

"We've got to do something!" Dash blurted.

Cocoa twirled her finger around one of her long curls. "I need to go get those eggs back!" She stood up and looked at her friends. They all looked shocked. "I can do it. I can trick that sour old troll!" she said. She stomped her foot. "He'd better watch out. No one steals candy from Cocoa the Chocolate Fairy!"

"No!" Raina blurted out. "No fairy has ever been on the other side of the Frosted Mountains! Our magic doesn't work over there."

"You don't know that for sure," Berry pointed out.

"Come on, Raina," Cocoa said. "We don't know if all those stories are true."

Raina's eyes grew wide with panic. "You don't believe the Fairy Code Book? Are you nuts?" Raina, unlike her friends, had memorized the Fairy Code Book. She knew the entire history of Candy Kingdom, and she was quick to point out any dangers.

Melli put her hand on Raina's shoulder. "Raina has a point. Have you ever heard of any fairy going far beyond Chocolate River and over the Frosted Mountains?"

"Why would anyone want to?" Dash cracked. "Everything we need is here—well, except the eggs, I guess."

Cocoa closed her eyes. "Bittersweet chocolate,"

she moaned. "This is awful." Her wings drooped low on the ground.

"Don't dip your wings in syrup yet," Berry said calmly. "We can think of a plan."

"Yes," Cocoa agreed. She was starting to perk up a little. "A plan to get me to Mogu's bridge. I've got a few words for him."

Berry held up her hand. "All right, hold on," she said. "You can't just go flying out there by yourself."

Raina's face was full of concern. "A fairy can't take anything from under a troll's bridge without permission," she said. She noticed the surprised looks on her friends' faces. "You really haven't read the Fairy Code Book?" she asked.

Laughing, Berry shook her head. "We don't have to," she said. "We have you!"

"Very funny," Raina said. "But this is serious sugar."

"There's only one person who can help," Melli said gently. Her friends nodded in agreement. They were all thinking the same thing.

Cocoa knew exactly who Melli was thinking of, but she didn't want to say. How could she tell the sweet fairy princess such awful news?

"Princess Lolli has a heart of sugar," Raina reminded her. "She'll be able to help. She is the wisest fairy in the kingdom."

"They don't call her princess for nothing," Dash added.

Berry moved closer to Cocoa. "She's your best bet, Cocoa. If anyone can hatch a plan to get the eggs back, it's Princess Lolli."

Cocoa knew her friends were right. Princess

Lolli always knew what to do. But would the princess let her go to Black Licorice Swamp? Cocoa had to go rescue the eggs—even if it meant she had to cross the Frosted Mountains alone!

CHAPTER
6

A Chocolate Promise

The fairies took off in the air and headed to Candy Castle. They flew side by side. They were on a mission to help their friend Cocoa.

Cocoa felt so lucky to have such good, true friends. She hoped with all her heart that no one else noticed the empty chocolate nest. Facing the other Chocolate Fairies would be terrible. She had to get those eggs back from Mogu before the parade!

When they could see the tallest lollipops in Lollipop Landing, Cocoa slowed her wings.

"Wait, what should I say to the princess?" Cocoa asked her friends. She floated in the air, waiting for the fairies to reply. "She has to let me go save the eggs!"

Her friends gathered around her.

Melli took her hand. "You should tell Princess Lolli the truth," she told her. "That's the easiest thing to do."

"And the hardest," Berry added.

"We'll all be with you," Raina said, reaching out to hold her friend's hand.

Dash bobbed her head up and down. "We won't leave your side," she vowed. "Plus, not only is Princess Lolli the kindest fairy, she's the smartest. She'll know what to do."

"Come on," Melli said. She squeezed Cocoa's hand, and together they flew off.

Cocoa was thankful for Melli's warm grip. While she wasn't afraid to find Mogu, she couldn't help being nervous about telling Princess Lolli what had happened. How would the princess react? She had put her trust in Cocoa. And Cocoa had made a solid chocolate promise to care for the eggs. Now that promise was broken.

"Everything will be okay," Melli said, looking over at Cocoa. "Princess Lolli won't be mad. She'll know this isn't your fault. Don't worry."

"We're almost there," Raina called out.

The bright pink castle came into view. With

her friends by her side, Cocoa felt she could handle anything. She would simply tell the princess that she had to save the eggs!

In front of the castle the Royal Gardens were in full bloom. All the brightly colored candy looked gorgeous—and delicious!

The garden was the pride of Sugar Valley. There was a sampling of all the candy grown in the kingdom, from the smallest fruit chews to the largest peppermint sticks. It was a rainbow of colors and a sensational sight.

The Castle Fairies who took care of the Royal Garden candy were all busy at work. They didn't even look up to wonder why the five Candy Fairies were flying in through the sugarcoated gates.

"Good afternoon," a fairy guard said, greeting them. He wore the official white-and-pink castle uniform. He tipped his cap and smiled. "What brings you lovely fairies here today?"

"Hello," Cocoa responded bravely. "We're here to see Princess Lolli."

"Is she expecting you?" the guard asked. He eyed the five fairies carefully.

Cocoa was about to answer, but the words wouldn't come out. She was too embarrassed to admit that the precious eggs were gone! She didn't know what to say to the guard.

Berry stepped forward. She fluttered her long pink wings. "Cocoa is the Chocolate Fairy watching over the spring eggs," she said. "She needs to speak to the princess at once."

While Cocoa didn't like people speaking for her, she was very relieved that Berry had stepped in. She turned to her friend and smiled. She was thankful that her friend understood how hard this was for her.

The guard nodded his head, and two Royal Fairies blew their shiny caramel trumpets to announce their arrival. Then the guard lifted the heavy white chocolate gate, and the fairies flew inside.

Cocoa took a deep breath as her feet touched down on the red licorice bridge. As she and her friends crossed the chocolate moat, Cocoa grew even more concerned. She looked around at all the candy in the Royal Gardens. If Mogu was able to send the Chuchies over to get the chocolate eggs, what would stop him from taking more candy? The whole kingdom was in danger! She hoped with all her heart that this egg situation would be fixed. And that she could put a stop to Mogu's candy stealing.

7

A Dangerous Plan

The five fairies found Princess Lolli in the throne room watering a multi-flavored jelly bean plant. She looked up and smiled at her guests.

"Hello," Princess Lolli called. "What a nice surprise to see you all here today." She lifted the heavy leaves of the plant. Gently, she plucked

a few ripe beans. "Would you care for some fresh jelly beans? The green apple and grape are especially tasty."

Cocoa stepped forward. "No, thank you, Princess Lolli," she said. "We're here with some very bitter news."

Looking concerned, the princess placed the golden watering can down. She waved the fairies into her chamber. There was a pink throne bejeweled with little pieces of dazzling sugar candies, and there were pink velvet couches for visitors. "Come inside," she told them. "Tell me what has happened. You all have such sour faces!"

The fairies followed the princess into the room. Before they even sat down on the princess's regal couches, Cocoa blurted out, "The chocolate eggs have been stolen from the nest in Chocolate Woods!"

"Stolen?" Princess Lolli asked. She sat in her throne. Her face no longer showed a smile, but a frown.

"Yes, princess," Berry said. She moved closer to her. "Raina and I saw a bunch of Chuchies taking the eggs across the river."

The princess touched her wavy strawberry-colored hair. "Mogu," she whispered.

"That's what we think," Dash piped up.

"Oh, princess!" Raina cried out. "Cocoa wants to cross the Frosted Mountains! I told her that it wasn't safe, but she still wants to go!"

Cocoa smiled at Raina. She knew her friend was just nervous for her. "The eggs were my responsibility," Cocoa said bravely. "I made a promise to protect the eggs. I want to go get them back." She stood up and walked closer to the candy throne. "The chocolate eggs mean so much to all of Candy Kingdom," she pleaded. "The Egg Parade is in two days!"

Princess Lolli looked thoughtfully at Cocoa. "Traveling across the Frosted Mountains is a dangerous journey," she warned.

"I know," Cocoa replied. She lowered her head. "But I need to go. The eggs were my responsibility. And now the kingdom is in great danger!"

"Your magic may not be as strong on the other side of the mountains," Princess Lolli went on. She looked into Cocoa's sad brown eyes. "As we head over the Frosted Mountains, our magic gets weaker."

"I understand," Cocoa told her. "But I want

to get those eggs back. We need to put a stop to Mogu's stealing."

The five fairies waited for the princess to respond. They gathered around Cocoa, holding hands. They stood in silence as they watched the princess decide.

The beautiful fairy princess looked out the large window of her chambers. She was deep in thought. When she finally turned back to look at them, she chose her words carefully.

"Mogu can't get away with stealing our candy," Princess Lolli said, full of determination. "We have to put a stop to this."

"I was hoping you'd say that," Cocoa said. She smiled at the princess.

"We will go together," Princess Lolli told her.

"Just the two of us. The trip is too dangerous to take you all."

Cocoa's friends looked worried. They wanted to help too. But Princess Lolli's decision was final.

Cocoa clapped her hands. *"Choc-o-rific!"* she cheered. "Wait till I get my hands on Mogu. . . ."

Princess Lolli held up her hand. "Wait," she said. "You will need to follow my every word. The only way to get what we want is to trick Mogu. Tricking an old troll like Mogu is sticky business. We will have to be clever and wise."

Cocoa nodded her head. "I understand," she told the princess.

"Mogu has tried to steal candy before," Princess Lolli said. "But he has never stolen chocolate eggs."

"I guess now he's got the Chuchies to do his dirty work for him," Berry said.

"All the more reason to teach him a lesson before the Chuchies become a bigger problem," Princess Lolli told them.

Raina took a map from her bag. "Here," she said. She gave the old scroll to the princess. "It's a map I drew of the Frosted Mountains. I memorized the locations from the Fairy Code Book. I hope it helps you reach Black Licorice Swamp safely."

Princess Lolli touched Raina's head gently. "Thank you," she said. "That map will be very useful." She looked each fairy in the eye. "I don't want all the fairies in the kingdom to panic," she explained. "This needs to remain a secret for now.

Can I count on all of you to keep this quiet?"

The fairies all nodded their heads solemnly.

"We will be back before Sun Dip," the princess said. "And, hopefully, we will return with the chocolate eggs."

Cocoa wanted to believe the princess. She hoped that by going on this journey, they would get the eggs back. And stop Mogu from stealing more from the fairies. It was a dangerous plan. Now more than ever she knew she had to be brave.

CHAPTER 8

Black Licorice

"Are you ready, Cocoa?" Princess Lolli asked. She stood at the back chocolate gate of the Candy Castle.

Cocoa nodded her head. She had no idea what the journey would be like, or what would happen. She hugged each of her friends.

"Be safe," Raina told her.

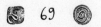

"Watch your wings," Berry advised. "Trolls are sneaky."

"Thanks," Cocoa said. She turned to Dash. "I'll see you soon."

"You better!" Dash called out.

Melli stood off to the side. She was trying to be brave like her friends. She didn't want to get all gooey; Cocoa wouldn't like that. Still, it was hard for her to be strong as she watched her friend fly into danger.

"We'll be all right," Cocoa told her. She gave Melli a tight squeeze. Cocoa didn't like to see her upset. "Save some of your caramel sticks for me," she said. "We'll be back for Sun Dip."

Melli managed to smile. "Sure as sugar," she whispered.

Princess Lolli reached out for Cocoa's hand.

Together, they flew off over the Royal Gardens to Red Licorice Lake. Cocoa watched as a bunch of fairies cared for the licorice growing around the cherry-red lake. They were all laughing as they trimmed the thick, sweet stalks.

As she flew, thoughts raced through her head. *What if we can't get the eggs back? What if something happens to Princess Lolli?*

When Peppermint Grove came into view, Cocoa tried to push those thoughts out of her head. She had to be strong. Chocolate River was up ahead. She had only been on the other side of the river once, last winter. She had gone to Marshmallow Marsh to gather filling for chocolate squares. The marsh was sticky, but not a scary place at all. Not like Black Licorice Swamp! Cocoa could feel her heart beating faster.

The rumbling of the river interrupted her thoughts. The flight over the river was quick. Cocoa looked down on the fluffy white peaks of Marshmallow Marsh. In a few quick wing strokes, they would be sailing up over the Frosted Mountains.

Cocoa looked at the princess. "What is the plan?" she asked.

Princess Lolli smiled and winked at the Chocolate Fairy. "We just need to stay true to our hearts. Salty old Mogu might be sneaky, but he isn't always wise."

Cocoa wanted to believe the princess. Still, she was unsure how the two of them could battle the old troll. In the stories she had heard as a young fairy, the troll was sneaky and strong. How could two small fairies be a match for him?

"Have you ever met Mogu?" Cocoa asked.

"Once," Princess Lolli replied. "I was a young fairy working with a crop of marshmallow blossoms at the edge of the marsh. Mogu thought he could trick me into giving him my basket of candy."

Cocoa flapped her wings to get closer to the princess. "Were you scared?"

"No," the princess said. "I knew I could outsmart him." She grinned and adjusted the silver crown on her head. "And I did!"

The Frosted Mountains were straight ahead. Cocoa took a deep breath.

"Remember," Princess Lolli told her, "our powers are not as strong on this side of the mountains. We will need to use our magic wisely."

Suddenly Cocoa felt dizzy. She closed her eyes for a second.

"Cocoa, hold on," Princess Lolli said, gripping Cocoa's hand tighter. "I know this trip is very difficult."

Feeling the princess's hand squeeze hers made her feel much better. All at once Cocoa had a burst of energy. When she opened her eyes again, she saw that the princess was smiling.

"The air here makes it hard for fairies to breathe," Princess Lolli said kindly. "But stay calm and you'll be fine. Come, let's head down to the swamp and find Mogu. Raina's map says this is the right direction."

Cocoa held tight to Princess Lolli's hand as they sailed over the Black Licorice Swamp. The smell of the thick, gooey swamp made her nose twitch. Everything around the swamp was black. Not at all like Red Licorice Lake. She longed to see the bright red stalks and wild berry candy bushes blooming along the Red Licorice Lake shores, and the happy Red Licorice Fairies harvesting the ripe stalks. Here at the dark, gloomy swamp there was no one in sight.

"Look over there!" Princess Lolli said, pointing.

The princess was pointing to a small bridge at the far end of the swamp. The bridge's black licorice bricks were covered in salt and didn't look very sturdy. Surrounding the bridge were tall, thin pretzel sticks. It looked like no one had cared for the pretzels—or the bridge—in years.

"There it is," Princess Lolli declared. "Mogu's

bridge. He's probably in his cave under the bridge."

"Let's go see," Cocoa said. She felt a new wave of energy and was ready to go.

"Wait," Princess Lolli told her. She held Cocoa back. "Remember, anything that is under the bridge cannot be removed without the troll's permission. We will need to be clever, and quick."

Cocoa nodded her head. "Yes, I remember," she said. She thought of her friends back in Sugar Valley, and tried to be as brave as Princess Lolli. "I'm ready."

Her head was still feeling strange, and Cocoa wondered if she could fly one more inch. But she knew that she had to keep going.

They flew down and hid behind a large black licorice stalk growing near the bridge. Carefully, they stepped over the rough salted pretzel sticks to get a better view of Mogu.

Cocoa gasped and drew her hands quickly up to her mouth. There was Mogu! His skin was wrinkled and dirty, and his clothes were torn. Just as all the stories described him, he was short and stout with white hair in a rim around his round head. And his large nose was sniffing one of Cocoa's chocolate eggs!

9

Chocolate Dreams

Princess Lolli and Cocoa stood together in the shadows of Mogu's bridge. The air was misty and cold, and the two fairies huddled close. Quietly, they peered around the salty old licorice bricks.

Cocoa couldn't believe how close she was to the troll! She found that she was less scared now that she saw him. She clutched her fists close to her side. She had to get those eggs back home!

Mogu was lying lazily on a hammock strung up under the bridge. The eggs were laid out in a black licorice basket before him.

Cocoa wanted to reach out and take the eggs, but she knew that she had to wait for Princess Lolli's instructions. She leaned closer to hear what Mogu was saying.

"Ah, I've missed the smell of chocolate," he grumbled. He rolled over and put his large nose next to the eggs and breathed deeply. "Ahhhh," he sighed.

Four Chuchies were sitting around the basket. Their round pom-pom bodies shook as they jumped up and down on their short, thin legs. "Meee, meee, meeeeeeeee," they chanted in a high-pitched squeal.

"Yes," Mogu said, petting one Chuchie. "I know you want to eat one." He grinned, showing off his black teeth. "You did a great job of getting these eggs over the mountains."

"Heee heee heeeeeeeeeeeee," the Chuchies cried out together.

Mogu looked pleased. "Yes, this was a ghoulish plan," he said. He shifted his weight in his hammock. "Those fairies never would have imagined that I could steal these eggs." His short arms rose up above his head. "Everyone knows spring eggs are the sweetest chocolate." He stretched happily. A sly grin spread across his face. "One day all the chocolate in the valley will be ours!"

Cocoa's eyes grew wide. How could Mogu be so cruel? She felt Princess Lolli squeeze her

hand. It was getting hard to stay quiet and listen to the mean troll.

"I've had enough of all those happy fairies and their sweetness in Sugar Valley," Mogu went on. He swung his short legs around to the side of the hammock and stood up. "This candy was so easy to take, just sitting in the nest! And no one was even watching! Why shouldn't we take more?"

Because we work hard to make the chocolate and all the candy in the valley, Cocoa wanted to scream. *Stealing is not the way to get candy!* She wanted to scold the troll. She bit her lip to keep quiet. Looking over at Princess Lolli, she wondered how the princess was remaining so calm. Now more than ever she wanted to reach out for the eggs.

"When I am the ruler of Candy Kingdom," Mogu bragged, "things will be different." He stomped his feet as he marched around the basket of eggs. He puffed his chest out. "I have big chocolate dreams." He kneeled down next to the basket. He stroked the eggs. "Hmmm," he said, sighing. Turning to the Chuchies, he grinned. "I will rule over the entire valley, my furry friends. And we will have all the chocolate that we could ever dream of! *Bah-ha-haaaaaaaa!*"

Bittersweet chocolate! Cocoa wanted to cry out. What would happen to all the sweet fairies in Sugar Valley if Mogu were in charge? What would happen to Candy Castle and Princess Lolli? This was all too horrible to think about. Defeated, Cocoa sank down to the soft, gooey ground of the swamp. What were they going to do?

Just then she felt a gentle squeeze on her shoulder. Princess Lolli was standing tall next to her. She had a slight grin on her face.

Cocoa knew that Princess Lolli had come up with a plan. She could tell from the sparkle in her eyes. But would the plan be strong enough to outwit this selfish troll? Would they be able to get the eggs safely home? Cocoa's wings fluttered. She was ready to do whatever the princess asked of her.

CHAPTER 10

A Touch of Chocolate

Princess Lolli waved Cocoa away from the bridge. They stood off to the side of the swamp so they could whisper.

"This is not your fault, Cocoa," Princess Lolli told her. "Mogu was wrong. And we will get the eggs back."

Cocoa wanted to believe the princess. She

nodded her head. All she wanted to do was protect those eggs from Mogu. A chocolate promise was a solid vow, and she wanted to be true to her word.

"When the time is right," Princess Lolli said, "I will signal to you." She looked into the fairy's sweet face. "You must concentrate and focus on your task. Because your magic is weaker on this side of the mountains, you need to rely on your heart."

Cocoa was not exactly sure what the princess was asking her to do. She could hardly even fly! But she wanted to help. She listened carefully.

"See the pretzel bramble over there?" the princess asked. She pointed behind Cocoa. "Do you think you can coat the stalks with chocolate?"

Cocoa wasn't sure she would be able to do as

the princess asked. Normally, she could touch anything and it would be covered in chocolate. But her head was spinning and there was a heaviness in her wings. Her magic was much weaker here. She didn't think she could create any chocolate!

Slowly Cocoa reached out to touch the pretzel stick. The pointy salt crystals were rough on her fingertips. Closing her eyes, she drew her breath in. When she opened her eyes, the salt was still there. There was not a drop of chocolate in sight. Cocoa's wings drooped low, and she looked down at her feet.

"Cocoa, you can do this," the princess told her. "Try again. Think of Chocolate Falls and Chocolate Woods. Listen to your heart."

This time Cocoa took a moment to think of her

home. She raised her head and closed her eyes. She thought of the ripples in Chocolate River and the rumbling sounds of Chocolate Falls. She imagined the dark bark of the old chocolate oak, and the tiny, strong chocolate branches of the egg nest. She remembered the sweet smell of chocolate rising throughout Sugar Valley on a beautiful spring day. Soon she imagined she could actually smell real chocolate.

"Oh, Cocoa!" Princess Lolli cried out.

Cocoa opened her eyes. The pretzels were now coated with rich, dark chocolate. Gently swaying in the breeze was a bunch of chocolate-covered pretzel sticks!

"You did it!" the princess said proudly. "I knew you had a solid chocolate heart!" She grinned. "You are a brave and true Candy Fairy, Cocoa."

The princess hugged her tightly. "Stay here until I call for you," she said.

In a flash, the royal fairy was gone.

Cocoa watched as the princess bravely stepped forward from the shadows of the bridge.

"Hello, Mogu," she said calmly. "I think you have something that belongs to Candy Kingdom."

Mogu turned his head, and Cocoa saw the surprised look on his face. "Well, well. Princess Lolli," he said. He quickly got over the shock of seeing the fairy princess and laughed. His laughter shook the whole bridge.

"What, these eggs? *Bah-ha-haaaaaaaa!* Your magic is no good here," he spat. "You know that you cannot move these eggs unless I allow it." He chuckled to himself. "And that is *not* going to

happen! I am in the mood for some chocolate."

The princess nodded her head knowingly. "Well then, I have something for you," she said. "Cocoa, show Mogu what you made." Bravely, Cocoa flew under the bridge with her arms full of the chocolate-covered pretzels.

Mogu's eyes grew big when he saw what the Candy Fairy was carrying. He took the sticks and shoved them all in his mouth. "Mmm," he said with his mouth full. "Salty and sweet! More! More!"

"As you wish," Princess Lolli said. She motioned for Cocoa to make more chocolate-covered pretzels.

The troll laughed. "You are going to give me candy?" he asked. He laughed as he reached out to grab the chocolate from Cocoa. "This is easier than I thought!"

The greedy troll kept on eating. Cocoa was getting weaker and weaker with each batch that she made. But the troll went on eating up all the chocolate treats. The Chuchies scurried around his feet, grabbing at all the crumbs that fell from his mouth. They were giddy with chocolate joy.

Cocoa wasn't sure why the princess was being so nice to Mogu. After all, he had stolen from them! Why would she want to give him more? But whatever the reason, she hoped with all her heart that the princess's chocolate plan worked.

CHAPTER 11

Dark Chocolate Wishes

Standing in the shadows of Mogu's cave, Cocoa watched. With Cocoa's help, the gentle fairy princess gave Mogu all the chocolate-covered pretzel sticks he wanted. Now his face was stained with chocolate. His hands were covered in a melted brown mess. The more he grabbed the chocolate and shoved it in his mouth, the more the princess grinned—and the dirtier he became.

"Mmmm," Mogu hummed. "I want more! I want more!"

Cocoa trusted Princess Lolli, but she wondered why she was giving Mogu the chance to eat so much chocolate.

"When I rule Candy Kingdom," he boasted, "I will make sure there are plenty of these salty chocolate treats. Thanks for the idea, princess! *Bah-ha-haaaaaaaa!*"

Mogu's evil laugh ruffled Cocoa's wings. She leaned against the bridge's salty black licorice bricks. Making the chocolate had taken most of her energy. And being on the far side of the Frosted Mountains was taking a toll on her. She tried hard to stand quiet and still.

Cocoa looked over at Princess Lolli. The brave princess was standing next to Mogu's hammock, watching him stuff himself with the chocolate treats. She caught Cocoa's eye and winked.

Then Cocoa heard the cry.

"Oooooooh," moaned Mogu. He stumbled back toward his hammock.

Princess Lolli moved out of the way.

Mogu sat down. His hands were on his bulging belly. "Ooooh, my tummy," he wailed.

The Chuchies crowded around him. "Mee, mee, meeeeeeeeeee?" they chanted together.

Princess Lolli offered him another bundle of chocolate-covered pretzels. Mogu waved his hand in front of his face. "Let me be!" he shouted. He moaned louder. "No more chocolate!" he mumbled. He closed his eyes and leaned back in the hammock.

"Mee, mee, *MEEEEEEEEE*?" the Chuchies asked a little louder.

Cocoa moved closer to Princess Lolli to get a better look. The damp cave now smelled like chocolate. Princess Lolli held up her hand, signaling Cocoa to wait.

"Argh!" the troll barked. He opened one eye. He peered over at the stack of chocolate pretzel sticks lying on the floor. He pushed the pretzels and the basket of eggs away with his foot.

"No more chocolate! Take all the chocolate away! I don't want to see chocolate under his bridge anymore!"

The Chuchies jumped up and got to work. When Mogu gave an order, they moved!

Princess Lolli stepped back and took Cocoa's hand. The Chuchies lifted the chocolate egg basket. They set the basket on the muddy ground—away from the bridge.

The eggs were no longer under the bridge!

Princess Lolli and Cocoa had tricked the troll without his realizing! He had ordered the eggs to be moved from under his bridge.

"Mogu," Princess Lolli said softly. She walked over to the hammock, where the troll was groaning softly.

"Is he asleep?" Cocoa whispered. She

peered over Princess Lolli's shoulder.

"Not quite," the princess told her. "But he will be in a chocolate coma for a while. He ate more than his fair share of chocolate today. His greed was almost as big as his appetite!"

Cocoa giggled. "And he had a very big appetite!"

"Oh, my tummy," Mogu cried out. He rolled over uncomfortably in his hammock.

Princess Lolli leaned in closer to him. "Nothing good comes of stealing, Mogu," she said.

Mogu moaned again.

"The sweet candy that you had today was freely given to you, and therefore the best kind," Princess Lolli told him. "But be warned," she said. "You must ask for candy, and never steal."

The Chuchies scrambled for all the chocolate

crumbs left spread around on the ground. They didn't look up as Princess Lolli and Cocoa slipped away from the bridge.

Princess Lolli turned to Cocoa. "Come, let's get the eggs back to the nest," she said. "Mogu won't be bothering us for a while now."

"Are you sure?" Cocoa asked. She looked back at the troll.

Mogu grunted and rolled over. "No more chocolate," he muttered in his sleep. "No more . . ." Soon he was snoring heavily.

"Yes," Princess Lolli said, smiling. She took both of Cocoa's hands and held them tight. "You were very brave today, Cocoa. I am so proud of you. I know it wasn't easy for you to make those chocolate pretzel sticks. That took strength and courage."

Cocoa blushed. "Thank you, princess," she said. "I can't help but feel this was my fault. I gave you my promise to take care of these eggs. Plus, I couldn't let Mogu take over Sugar Valley!"

"And he won't," Princess Lolli said. "At least, not today!" Her eyes sparkled. "Best to trick a troll with sweetness," she added. "There are other ways, but this is the surest."

The two fairies hugged.

"Come, let's bring the eggs home," Princess Lolli said. "We'll be back just in time for Sun Dip."

Together, they lifted the basket and flew the eggs back to the chocolate nest.

CHAPTER
12

Solid Chocolate

Wow!" Melli whispered to Cocoa. "Everything does look *choc-o-rific*! You saved the day,
Cocoa."

Cocoa and her friends stood on a stage built
of white chocolate in the Royal Gardens. A large
white banner hung across the stage. WELCOME,
SPRING! was written in pink icing letters. Huge

baskets of delicious candy flowers and thick red licorice stalks made the stage a beautiful sight. Everyone in the Royal Gardens was waiting for the Egg Parade to reach the castle. And to get a glimpse of the chocolate eggs!

Cheers were heard throughout the kingdom as the Chocolate Fairies marched in the festive parade. Some fairies rode on large floats made of chocolate, from the darkest dark to the purest white chocolate. On each float there were fairies showing off the season's chocolate treats. Other Chocolate Fairies marched alongside the floats, waving and throwing out candy to the crowd.

The cheers brought a smile to Cocoa's face. The Egg Parade was a big success, and the prized eggs were definitely the highlight.

"Everything does look *choc-o-rific*!" Cocoa said,

smiling. She looked around at her friends. "Sure as sugar this wouldn't have happened if it weren't for all of you."

"We didn't do anything," Dash said. "You were the one who saved the kingdom!"

"No fairy has ever been able to create candy in Black Licorice Swamp!" Raina cried.

Berry laughed. "Not that any fairy would want to!"

"The fact is that you did save the eggs," Melli said. "You are a hero, Cocoa!"

"And I have the sweetest friends," Cocoa added. She reached out to hug her friends. "You all came to help. You dropped everything and came to Chocolate Woods. You gave me the courage to go to Princess Lolli. How can I ever thank you?"

"That's what friends do," Raina said simply.

"Sure as sugar, they do!" Melli said, hugging Cocoa. "We are all very proud of you. Really."

"And Princess Lolli," Cocoa added. She looked over at the beautiful fairy princess. She was wearing her crown iced with the prized royal jewels, and her bright pink regal robe. "You should have seen her. She was so clever. She never gave in to that salty old troll! Her plan worked perfectly."

Just then the caramel trumpets blared. Everyone looked to the royal gates. The candy procession slowly made its way up a special red walkway made of the finest strawberry and raspberry candies. The Chocolate Fairies all beamed with pride as they walked to the stage.

Princess Lolli sat tall in her dazzling candy throne in the middle of the stage. The Royal

Fairies had worked so hard to make the castle sparkle, and everything was perfect. Princess Lolli waved Cocoa over to her.

Cocoa flew over excitedly.

"It's almost time," Princess Lolli said. She smiled warmly at the Chocolate Fairy. "Are you ready, Cocoa?"

"I am," Cocoa said, full of pride. She leaned in closer and whispered in her ear, "Thank you, princess."

Cocoa stood tall next to Princess Lolli's throne. She straightened her special chocolate leaf crown on her head. She was ready. Feeling like her heart would burst with happiness, she tried to keep her wings still.

Four Chocolate Fairies carried a large sugar basket up to the stage. A chocolate quilt covered the spring eggs inside.

Princess Lolli stepped to the front of the stage. "Welcome to the annual Egg Parade!" she announced. She smiled at the crowd of fairies that filled the Royal Gardens.

The fairies all cheered.

"It is with great pride that I call upon Cocoa, our bravest Chocolate Fairy," she said. "She has the honor of unveiling the prized spring chocolate eggs. Without her bravery, strength, and solid chocolate heart, we would not have these special eggs to celebrate today!"

An excited roar erupted from the crowd. The fairies were chanting Cocoa's name. Word had spread quickly of Cocoa's bravery. Everyone in Sugar Valley knew how Cocoa had made chocolate-covered pretzels appear in the Black Licorice Swamp and how she had helped put an end to Mogu's plan. The chanting grew louder as she reached the center of the stage.

Cocoa stood next to Princess Lolli, waving to the crowd. Then she looked back over her shoulder. Her friends were cheering. Never had she been so proud!

She took hold of the chocolate blanket covering the sugar basket. With a gentle tug the blanket came off. Sparkling in the bright sunlight were the chocolate eggs. They were wrapped in the special foil covers created by the Royal Foil Fairies. The brightly colored designs were bold and beautiful. Each one had a unique design. The Royal Foil Fairies had done a fantastic job. The eggs were a delicious sight!

The crowd gasped. This was the highlight of the Egg Parade! And no one was happier than Cocoa.

"Cheers for Cocoa!" Princess Lolli declared. "Her bravery and her dedication to these eggs are reasons to celebrate. Happy Spring to all the fairies of Sugar Valley!"

The cheers brought a huge smile to Cocoa's face.

"And now," the princess declared, "let the chocolate feast begin!"

"I thought she'd never say that!" Dash said happily. She flew off quickly to gather some of the chocolate treats.

"Come on," Berry urged her friends. "Let's check out the floats with all the chocolates!" She spread her pink wings and followed Dash.

Cocoa took Melli's and Raina's hands. "You heard the princess," she said. "Let's eat!"

Together, the three fairies flew after Dash and Berry into the crowd.

The caramel trumpets blasted once again. Spring had arrived—along with the most delicious chocolates ever grown in Sugar Valley.

Cocoa watched her friends enjoying the feast. They gathered around her, grinning. Standing together, they all felt the excitement of the day.

Candy Kingdom was safe from Mogu—for now, at least. And that was definitely a reason for a sweet celebration.

Rainbow Swirl

For Emily Lawrence,

an editor sure as sugar!

Contents

CHAPTER 1   Gummy Dreams   119

CHAPTER 2   Sun Dip Treats   131

CHAPTER 3   Candy Spirit   143

CHAPTER 4   Sweet Sign-up   153

CHAPTER 5   Bitter Words   166

CHAPTER 6   A Sour Sight   176

CHAPTER 7   A Berry Surprise   188

CHAPTER 8   Candy Fair   196

CHAPTER 9   Tasty Tastings   206

CHAPTER 10   The Sweetest Award   214

CHAPTER
1

Gummy Dreams

Raina, a Gummy Fairy, grinned as she flew over Gummy Forest. Sweet, fruity smells filled the air as she glided down into the forest. She loved the colorful gummy trees and gummy wildflowers that filled her home. From the sky above, the forest was a beautiful rainbow patchwork.

"Lunchtime!" Raina sang out. She swooped down to Gummy Lake in the middle of the forest.

Raina was in charge of taking care of the gummy animals. All of the animals, from the adorable gummy bears to the mischievous gummy fish, loved her. Her kind and patient nature made her perfect for the job.

"Come and eat," Raina called. She flew over Gummy Lake, sprinkling flavor flakes in the water for the fish.

A swarm of bright red, green, yellow, and orange gummy fish surfaced and gobbled up the food.

Every day at the same time Raina would give the gummy fish their flavor flakes. The Fairy Code stated that gummy fish needed one serving of flavoring a day. Raina had memorized the Fairy Code Book. Some of her fairy friends

made fun of her for following the rules so closely. Berry, a Fruit Fairy, and Dash, a Mint Fairy, were not big on following codes and rules. But Raina liked order and rules.

After giving the gummy fish their lunch, Raina poured the rest of the flavor flakes into a hollowed-out gummy log for the gummy bears. Then she poured in some sweet syrup to make a sticky mixture. She rubbed her hands on her dress. A few more flavor flakes stuck on her dress wouldn't matter. Her dress already had every color of the rainbow!

Raina was named after the Great Rainbow that appeared the day she was born. Because she was born under the rainbow, she loved bright colors—which was part of the reason she loved Gummy Forest so much.

She blew a few notes on her red candy whistle, and the little gummy bears came out of their caves. The cheerful little bears all lined up at the tree to get a scoop of their sticky treat. Raina made extra sure their food mixture was as sweet as honey.

The bears all reached out their paws to get their share. A little red bear slurped down his portion quickly.

"Slowly," Raina said gently. She patted the little red cub on the head. "Nokie, I know that you're hungry, but there's plenty here."

The red bear took his scoop and then waddled over to the gummy tree to lick his paws.

Raina smiled at the line of cute bears. Of all the gummy animals, she liked the gummy bear cubs the best. With their plump bellies and jolly personalities, the bears were fun to be around. Especially little Nokie.

Raina looked over at the tree behind her to see the young cub eating. Nokie was always first in line for feedings. Raina smiled at the bright red cub. Then she tucked her long, straight dark hair behind her ears and began to scoop out the food for each of the bears.

"Hi, Raina!" Berry called out. The Fruit Fairy flew down through the gummy trees and landed next to her friend. "I thought I would find you here." She pointed to the line of bears. "I see it's feeding time," she said, smiling. Berry liked the gummy cubs too.

"Right on schedule," Raina replied happily. She grinned at the beautiful Fruit Fairy. Berry's raspberry-colored dress wasn't stained or creased, like Raina's dress. And sparkly sugarcoated fruit-chew clips held her hair in a perfect bun. Berry always looked her best.

"What brings you to Gummy Forest?" Raina asked.

Berry reached into the bag that was slung around her shoulder. "I am delivering some fresh strawberry syrup," she replied. She held out a jar. When the sun hit it, the red liquid inside glowed. "I just made the syrup this morning. It's *berry* fresh," she said, giggling.

"Perfect," Raina replied. "I'm sure Miro will be happy to have that. She's over by the gummy flower patch." She pointed to the young Gummy Fairy watering a bunch of seedlings. "She'll be glad to get the new flavor for the flower garden."

"Thanks," Berry said. She put the jar back in her bag for safekeeping.

When the last gummy bear had his serving, Berry helped Raina clean up. Together, they carried the gummy bears' feeding log over to the lake to wash it.

"Have you decided what you are going to make for Candy Fair this year?" Berry asked as she scrubbed the inside of the log clean.

Raina nodded her head quickly. Candy Fair was all she had been thinking about! She had been doing research, trying to find just the right new candy to make for the fair.

"I want to make a new candy," Raina replied. "Something extraordinary!"

Candy Fair was a spring event that was held every four years at the Candy Castle. All the

fairies throughout Sugar Valley displayed their candy in the Royal Gardens. White tents were set up, and each fairy had a booth to show her candy. Fairy Princess Lolli was the fairy who ruled over Candy Kingdom, and she sampled all the candy. The princess and her Royal Fairy advisers gave the fairy with the best candy the honor of the sugar medal. They had a difficult job, but they each had a very good sense of taste and were extremely fair.

This year Raina wanted that medal more than anything. It would be the first year that she was competing. Four years ago she was not old enough. But this year was a different story. This year she not only wanted to show candy, she wanted to win.

Raina had another reason for wanting to win

so badly. No Gummy Fairy had ever won the sugar medal. In all the books that Raina had read, she couldn't find one time that a Gummy Fairy had received the first-place honor. The medal usually went to a Chocolate Fairy, and there were a few years that other fairies had won. But never a Gummy Fairy. This seemed unfair to Raina. This year Raina vowed to make the outcome of Candy Fair different.

"I want to be the first Gummy Fairy to win the sugar medal!" Raina exclaimed. She grinned at her friend. She hoped her dream of winning would come true. "What about you? Have you decided what you are going to make?"

Berry spread her pink wings. "I'm not sure," she said. She looked down at her sparkly shoes. "We'll see."

"We always said that we'd all make candy for the fair," Raina said. She shook her head in disbelief. "How could you not make something?" she asked.

Berry looked down at the ground. She didn't answer Raina's question. She didn't have the right words. She knew how Raina felt about Candy Fair. The problem was that she didn't feel the same way.

Berry lifted up the end of the log and placed it on the ground. "So what are you going to make?" she asked, changing the subject. "You need to decide soon."

"I'm still doing research," Raina said. "But you can be sure as sugar that this year a Gummy Fairy is going to win Candy Fair!"

2

Sun Dip Treats

A few days later Raina flew quickly toward Red Licorice Lake. The large yellow sun was beginning to dip below the Frosted Mountains. Raina couldn't wait to see her friends. She was excited about a new gummy candy she had grown. She was carrying a sample of her new candy to Sun Dip.

Sun Dip was a time for all the fairies to nibble on candy and rejoice in another day in Sugar Valley. And maybe today try a new gummy candy that would win first prize at Candy Fair. Raina hoped her friends would like the new sweet treat.

The sky was full of swirls of orange, pink, and a touch of lavender. Sun Dip was Raina's favorite time of day. All the scents in Sugar Valley were the strongest in the early evening. The gentle winds blew sweet smells from all areas of the valley. Sun Dip was the perfect time for fairies to come together and visit. Work was done for the day, and all the fairies enjoyed the quiet time with their friends.

Raina and her friends gathered at the hill on Lollipop Landing near Fruit Chew Meadow.

On the hill the friends could sit and watch the sun dip below the mountains. Between the colorful lollipops and the rolling meadow full of fruit chews, the area was a favorite spot for the friends.

"Hi, Raina!" Melli called out, waving to her. The Caramel Fairy was sitting on a large, round purple fruit chew.

"Hi," Raina said. She landed next to her friend and held out her basket. She couldn't wait for Melli to have a taste.

"Oh, what did you bring?" Melli asked. She looked into the basket.

"Try some of my new gummy berries," Raina told her. She took the cloth off her basket to show Melli. The basket was full of all different colors of strawberry-shaped gummy berries.

"You grew these?" Melli said, and gasped. "Raina, these look sensational. I've never seen so many different colors of berries."

"Taste one," Raina said. "I hope you'll like them." She handed Melli a bright blue berry.

As soon as Melli popped the berry in her mouth, her eyes grew wide. "Sweet sugar!" she cried. "This is delicious!"

Raina beamed with pride. She knew the strawberry-shaped candy looked pretty. But in order to win the sugar medal, the candy had to taste good too.

"Is this what you are going to show at Candy Fair?" Melli asked. "They look like strawberries, but they don't taste like strawberries. And so many colors! This one was very tasty."

"Thank you," Raina said. "I've been researching,

and I can't find any other gummy berries in the Fairy Code Book." She pulled a stack of books from her bag. "Actually, I haven't been able to find any gummy berries in any of these books."

Melli glanced at the pile of books in front of Raina. She kept pulling more and more books out of her bag: *Fairy Foods*, *The Joy of Sugar*, *Gummy Gigi's Treats*, and *Berry Delicious Sweets*.

"You've certainly done your research," Melli said, nodding her head. She stared at the tall stack of books in front of Raina.

"Where's Cocoa?" Raina asked. She looked around for the Chocolate Fairy.

Cocoa the Chocolate Fairy would never sugarcoat the truth. If she didn't like the candy, she would tell Raina.

"Right behind you," Cocoa said, laughing. She tapped Raina on the shoulder.

Raina should have known that wherever Melli was, Cocoa wasn't far behind. The two fairies were always together.

"Hi, Cocoa," Raina said. She loved Cocoa's long dark curls. Her own dark hair was just as long, but it was stick straight.

Cocoa peered inside Raina's basket. "What did you bring?" she asked. "Gummy berries?"

"Yes, they are all different-flavored berries. I changed strawberries into flavored gummy berries!" Raina declared.

"She's going to show them at Candy Fair," Melli added.

"Chocolate sprinkles, Raina!" Cocoa exclaimed. "Melli and I haven't even thought of what we're

going to do yet. And you already have your candy!"

"Well, I've been trying out some new things," Raina confessed. She held out the basket to her friend. "Try one."

Raina waited as Cocoa popped one in her mouth. She watched as Cocoa swished the candy around her mouth and then swallowed.

"Well?" Raina asked. She couldn't stand waiting!

"Choc-o-rific!" Cocoa shouted.

Fluttering her red wings, Raina raised her feet off the ground. "Really? You like them?"

Cocoa nodded her head. "Good work," she said. "Did you find these in one of your books?"

"No," Raina said. "I wanted to make sure no one had ever created these candies before. The best chance for the sugar medal is to come up with something totally new."

Melli and Cocoa shared a look. When Raina got focused on a task, she had a one-track fairy mind.

"Hello, fairies," Dash greeted her friends. Most Mint Fairies were small, but Dash was the smallest in Sugar Valley. Though she was tiny, she had a big personality—and appetite. She straightened her white dress and settled down to snack on some of Cocoa's chocolate squares.

"Slow down," Cocoa said, laughing. "I brought those for everyone to share."

Dash giggled. "Sorry!" she said. She licked her fingers. "These are my favorites, you know."

"Dash, you say that about every candy!" Melli said, smiling. Then she noticed a small rip in Dash's dress. "Dash, what happened to your dress?" she asked.

"Oh, it's nothing," Dash said. She fluttered her silver wings. "I just got it caught when I was testing out my new sled."

"Sled?" Cocoa asked. "It's springtime, Dash! Haven't you noticed?"

"Winter is a long time away," Raina added.

Dash shrugged. She loved marshmallow sledding. She had won the Sugar Valley sledding competition two years in a row. Winter couldn't come fast enough for her.

"Yum, what are those?" Dash asked. She peered inside Raina's basket of gummy berries.

"Try one," Raina said. She held the basket up for Dash to take a berry.

"Holy peppermint!" Dash cried after she

ate one. "These are yummy. Where'd you find them?"

Spreading her wings proudly, Raina smiled. "I grew them especially for Candy Fair."

"Nice job," Dash said, reaching for another.

Raina looked up in the sky. "Where's Berry?" she asked. "I wanted her to try one."

Usually Berry was the last fairy to arrive since she took the longest to get ready. But the sun was already down. Sun Dip would be over very soon.

"I'm sure she'll be here soon," Melli said. She put her hand on Raina's shoulder. "You know Berry is always late."

"Can I have another one of those berries?" Dash asked.

Raina smiled. She held out her basket. She was feeling good about her candy, but she wanted one more opinion. She looked to the sunset sky, hoping to see Berry . . . soon.

CHAPTER
3

Candy Spirit

I see Berry," Raina said, squinting. She pointed up in the darkening sky.

"I wonder what she's got in her basket?" Dash asked, looking up. "Maybe she has a new candy for the fair too."

"Oh, Dash," Melli said, laughing.

"Or maybe she's bringing some fruit leather!"

Dash said excitedly. She jumped to her feet. Her large blue eyes were sparkling. "Those are my favorite."

Melli, Cocoa, and Raina all laughed. Every candy was Dash's favorite.

"Hi, everyone," Berry said cheerfully. "I've got to show you these amazing fruit chews." Before she even landed on her feet, she was showing off her sparkling candy jewels. "This new crop is the best ever. Look at these!"

"Oh, Berry," Melli said, looking at the candy. "These are beautiful. You're right. These are all supersparkly."

"Are you going to show those at Candy Fair this year?" Raina asked.

Berry started to laugh. "Sweet sugar!" she cried. "These are not for eating." She scooped up the candy and placed the jewels back in her basket. "These are going to be the jewels in my new necklace."

"I don't know," Dash said, looking over. "They look good enough to eat."

Berry rolled her eyes, and then a smile spread across her face. "Everything looks good enough for *you* to eat, Dash!"

"I'm serious," Raina said. "The rules of Candy Fair aren't only about the best-tasting candy. You can get an honorable mention for color and shape as well."

"Leave it to Raina to know *all* the rules of Candy Fair," Cocoa said. She sat down on a hard candy rock and took a sip of sugar nectar from a nearby flower.

"It's true," Raina told her friends. She folded

her arms across her chest. "The candy just needs to be created by a fairy." She grinned at Berry. "I think you should show these at the fair. Everyone will love them."

Berry flapped her wings and sat down on the red sprinkle sand. "I'll think about it," she said. She sighed heavily. "I'm not sure I'm going to show anything at the fair."

"What?" Raina said. She couldn't believe her ears. "What do you mean, you're not going to show candy at the fair? It's all we've talked about for the past four years! It's everyone's dream to win the sugar medal at Candy Fair!"

Berry shrugged. She looked down at her toes. "It's all *you've* talked about," she said softly. "It's *your* dream." Then she picked up some sprinkles in her hand and let the tiny grains fall through

her fingers. "I'm just not sure that I want to compete. I've been busy with my jewelry."

"Melli and I are going to work together," Cocoa said, stepping between them. "We're going to do a caramel and chocolate candy." She turned and fluttered her wings with Melli.

"What about you, Dash?" Melli asked. "I'm sure you have some minty surprise blooming."

Dash shook her head. "No, I haven't had time. I'm too busy building a new sled for the marshmallow slopes."

"What's in your basket, Raina?" Berry asked. She pointed to the basket next to her friend.

Raina had almost forgotten to ask Berry to try her new candy. She held out the basket. "These are my new gummy berries for Candy Fair," she told her.

"May I try one? They look good," Berry said.

As she handed the candy to Berry, Raina couldn't help but feel a swirl of sadness surround her.

She couldn't understand how Berry and Dash didn't want to compete. She had thought all her friends were just as excited as she was about the upcoming candy event. Didn't they have the candy spirit too? She never imagined going to the fair without all her friends. Suddenly, going to Candy Fair didn't seem as sweet to her. . . .

Melli noticed the sad look on Raina's face. "Don't worry, Raina," Melli said. She came over to her and put her arm around her. "Cocoa and I are going to the sign-up for the fair tomorrow

at Candy Castle. Why don't we meet up and go together?"

Raina smiled, thankful for Melli's excitement. "Yes," she said. "Let's get there early. I want to make sure to be one of the first fairies to sign up for the fair."

"That's the spirit," Cocoa said, jumping up.

"These gummy berries are scrumptious," Berry said. She reached for another one from Raina's basket. "And I love how colorful the sweets are. You have a berry flavor for every color of the rainbow!"

Raina smiled. Berry had noticed the one thing she was most proud of. Maybe her candy really could win the sugar medal! She spread her wings. Suddenly she had even more candy spirit bubbling up inside of her. Even though she was disappointed that Berry and Dash were not competing, she had to focus. She'd have to concentrate if she was going to win . . . with or without her friends.

4

Sweet Sign-up

Raina set out for the Royal Gardens very early the next morning. The sun was just rising over the pink-and-white Candy Castle, and all of Sugar Valley was still. To Raina, the air smelled especially good this spring morning. Springtime was her favorite season in Sugar Valley. So many of the candy trees, bushes, and flowers were in bloom. Even the lollipop trees had sprouted by the royal gates, making the entrance to the castle more grand than on a normal day. With more candy in bloom and the added decoration, the castle looked ready for Candy Fair. Raina sighed as she took a deep breath. She had been waiting for this for four long years!

She waved when she spotted Melli and Cocoa just outside the royal gates. But much to Raina's surprise, the three of them weren't the first fairies there.

"Sour sticks!" Raina cried. She saw the long line of fairies waiting. "I thought we'd be the first fairies here!"

Melli flew up right behind her. "This isn't a race, Raina," she said. She put her hand on Raina's shoulder. "Besides, the line isn't that long."

"I suppose," Raina said, looking around. She looked up at the sky. "I guess Berry and Dash really aren't going to come after all," she said sadly.

"Just because they aren't showing candy this year doesn't mean they won't come to the fair," Melli told her.

"I know," Raina said, brushing her foot on the ground. "I just hope they'll change their minds."

"Maybe," Cocoa said. She looked toward the Candy Castle. "I wonder if Princess Lolli is here," she said.

Princess Lolli and Cocoa had recently gone on a journey over the Frosted Mountains to Black Licorice Swamp. Mogu, the sour old troll who lived there, had stolen Cocoa's chocolate eggs. The two fairies took a dangerous journey to see him. Since that time, Cocoa and Princess Lolli had shared a special bond.

"Of course she's here!" Raina replied. "How could she not be here for Candy Fair sign-up? Candy Fair is the most important candy event."

Cocoa shrugged. "Not to every Candy Fairy," she said.

Raina's eyes opened wide. "What are you talking about?" she said. "Candy Fair is one of the greatest candy events. Besides, it's a huge honor. Every fairy knows that Princess Lolli decides who gets the sugar medal. "

"Princess Lolli *and* her royal advisers," Melli added.

Raina felt her face getting red. Why weren't her friends taking this event more seriously? Didn't they realize the importance of the fair?

"You don't have to get your wings in a flutter," Cocoa told her. "I was just saying . . ."

Melli stepped in between her friends. "Look, we're next in line," she said cheerfully. "You see, the wait wasn't long after all."

The three fairies moved up closer to the middle of the garden. There was a long white table set up between the rows of chocolate oaks. Tula, a trusted Royal Fairy adviser to Princess Lolli, was writing down on a giant scroll the name of every fairy who signed up.

"Come on," Raina said, pulling her friends along. She had read about Tula in her books, and she was anxious to meet her. She was a Gummy Fairy too. But now she lived in the castle with Princess Lolli.

Raina couldn't wait to tell Tula about her new

berries. She hoped she'd like them. And that she could win Tula's vote for the best candy at Candy Fair.

As Raina got closer to the sign-up table, her wings started to flutter. She was so nervous! She had been dreaming of creating a new candy for the fair for so long. And now she was going to present her candy idea. She couldn't believe this was actually happening.

"Name?" Tula asked. She didn't even look up from the large scroll in front of her. In her hand was a large feather that she dipped in a small tub of red syrup for ink.

Raina looked over at her two friends. They pushed her forward toward the table. But Raina was too nervous to speak.

"I'll go first," Cocoa said. She stepped in front

of Raina. "My name is Cocoa the Chocolate Fairy, and this is my friend Melli the Caramel Fairy. We'd like to make chocolate-caramel lollipops."

"We're calling them friendship pops," Melli added.

Tula wrote down the entry on the scroll with her feather pen. "Very well," she said. "Nice to see you working together."

"Thank you," Melli said, smiling.

"Good luck," Tula said. Then she looked up at Raina. "Next?"

"My name is Raina," she said quietly. "I am a Gummy Fairy." She felt her heart beating quickly and her wings fluttering. She had to will herself to stay firmly on the ground as she spoke.

"What will you be presenting at Candy Fair

this year?" Tula asked. She peered over her sparkly glasses.

Raina noticed that there were tiny speckles of sugar crystals along the frames of Tula's glasses. The older fairy also wore a thick, woven red licorice bracelet on her right wrist. Her white hair was swept up in a fancy swirl on the top of her head, and her red dress sparkled in the sun. She was beautiful.

"Sweetie, do you have a candy idea?" Tula asked gently. Her deep blue eyes were kind, and she smiled warmly at Raina.

Immediately Raina felt better. "I'd like to introduce a new gummy candy," she said. Suddenly she had a burst of confidence as she thought of her candy project.

Tula pushed her glasses up on her nose.

"A new gummy candy?" she said. She looked right into Raina's dark eyes. "Very nice. What is the candy called?" She held the feather next to the scroll.

Raina didn't know what to say! She hadn't thought of a name for her candy!

Cocoa leaned in close to them. "They are yummy gummy berries," she said, smiling at Raina. "Each berry is a different color and flavor."

Tula nodded her head. "I see," she said. With careful strokes, she wrote the entry next to Raina's name in fancy script. "That sounds challenging," she added.

"I've done lots of research," Raina explained. "I have everything all planned out. In my garden each berry bush is a different flavor. The berries will be just perfect."

The older fairy shook her head. "Oh, Raina," she said. "The best candy is not always perfect."

"What do you mean?" Raina asked. She had followed all the rules and had carefully planted the bushes. She was taking excellent care of the plants. She was certain that no Gummy Fairy had ever tried to grow berries like the ones she had. They would be perfect.

"Sometimes the greatest surprises come from the most unlikely places," Tula advised. She smiled at the three fairies standing in front of her. "Good luck with your berries," she said with a wink.

"What do you think she meant?" Raina asked Cocoa and Melli as they flew through the Royal Gardens.

"I'm not sure," Melli said. "But I'm looking forward to the fair. Look at all these fairies here for the sign-up!" She pointed to the long line that snaked through the castle gates.

"Competition will be tough," Cocoa said. A smile spread across her face. "I can't wait!"

"Me neither," Raina gushed. She felt happy after officially signing up for the fair. Now more than ever she wanted to prove that a Gummy Fairy could win the first-place prize at Candy Fair.

5

Bitter Words

Early the next morning Raina checked on her berry patch. She carefully watered the berry bushes and pruned the leaves. A little gummy bunny poked her head up from underneath one of the bushes.

"Hello," Raina said. She knelt down and scooped up the little bunny with her hand. "What

do you think about these new berries, huh?" She stroked her orange head. "I know you want a bite, but these fruits are for Candy Fair," she told the bunny, "not for you." She carefully placed the bunny outside the fence. Then she plucked a bright purple leaf from another bush for the bunny to nibble on.

Raina closed the fence gate and looked over at the small gummy berry bushes.

Everything looks perfect, she thought happily.

Now that she had signed up for the fair, her plan was moving forward. She had a chance to win the sugar medal this year. She was sure her perfect plan was going to work!

Raina arrived at Chocolate River anxious to tell Berry and Dash about what had happened at Candy Castle. The sugar sand beach along

Chocolate River was their morning meeting spot. The friends tried to meet there every morning to share stories.

When Raina arrived, she was surprised to find Berry already on the sugar beach. The Fruit Fairy was leaning on a large candy rock and making a candy-chew necklace. By her side was a basket filled with sugarcoated jewels. The candies sparkled in the bright morning sun.

As Raina got closer, she saw that Melli and Cocoa were sitting next to Berry. They seemed to be involved in a very serious conversation. Her friends didn't even look up to see that she had flown in.

"Aren't you concerned about Raina?" Berry asked. "All she is talking about is Candy Fair."

"You mean *winning* the sugar medal *at* Candy

Fair," Cocoa corrected her. "I've never seen Raina so focused on something . . . that wasn't a book!"

"I know," Berry said. "I'm concerned about her."

Raina's wings drooped. While she knew that she shouldn't be listening to her friends' conversation, she was hurt that they were talking about her. She stepped out in front of them.

"If you don't think I can win, you should just tell me," Raina stated.

Her three friends all looked up. Berry looked startled. "I didn't see you, Raina," she said, moving closer to her. "I didn't mean that you can't win," she explained. "I'm just worried about you. All you seem focused on is winning the medal. What about enjoying the fair?"

Raina couldn't believe her ears. She flapped her wings and lifted herself up. "I'm leaving," she said. "I have to go over to Red Licorice Lake for some flavor crystals. Since Candy Fair isn't important to you, you wouldn't understand."

Berry looked to Melli and Cocoa. Raina knew her words were bitter, but she couldn't help feeling mad. Winning was important to her—very important.

"Wait," Berry pleaded.

But Raina had already flown off. She sped past Dash as she flew toward Red Licorice Lake.

Dash looked after her, confused. What had she missed?

"I've never seen Raina have such a sugar fit," Cocoa remarked, shaking her head.

"Where was she off to?" Dash asked. She

looked after her friend speeding away. "There's a terrible storm coming. All the fruit flies are buzzing about the high winds and rains."

Raina didn't look back. She didn't want to hear a weather report. She was on a mission. Her bushes needed more flavor crystals right away. Her friends just didn't understand. They weren't taking Candy Fair seriously at all! She'd show them who could win first place!

As Raina flew, she saw dark clouds moving quickly toward her. A tiny fruit fly buzzed around her ear, warning her of a dangerous storm. But Raina pressed on.

If I can just get the crystals quickly, she thought, *I'll make it back to Gummy Forest before the rains come!*

A few cool raindrops splashed her face. Raina flew faster. But then the sky turned a dark purple—a shade she had never seen.

"Head home," a fruit fly buzzed in her ear. "A terrible storm is coming."

Raina swatted the fly away and swooped down to the shore of Red Licorice Lake. As her feet touched the ground, the rain began to fall harder.

She had never seen so much rain! She took out a bottle and scooped up the flavor sprinkles for the berry bushes.

Then a strong gust of wind lifted Raina's feet off the ground. She was picked up and tossed into the air. She sailed across the lake and landed in a sticky web of licorice stalks. Her wings were caught in a tangle of licorice. She couldn't move. She was stuck!

Oh no, she thought.

As much as she tried, her wings wouldn't budge. She couldn't move. As she looked around at the storm whirling around her, she thought about her berry bushes.

I need to get home and protect them, she thought.

The more she struggled to free herself, the more she felt the pull on her wings.

Watching the rain beat down around her, Raina thought about how she had not prepared for the storm. She had not even put a cover over the bushes. Sure as sugar, those bushes would be destroyed.

All her hard work was going to be swirled away by the storm. Her eyes filled with tears.

"How did I let myself get into this sticky mess?" she wailed.

But no one was around to hear her. It seemed that all the other Candy Fairies had listened to the warnings the fruit flies were spreading. And now her perfect candy was going to be ruined. All her dreams of winning the sugar medal were washed away.

CHAPTER
❀ 6 ❀

A Sour Sight

Raina was miserable. She was soaking wet and still stuck in a sticky tangle of licorice vines.

Sure as sugar, my candy berry bushes are destroyed by now, she thought sadly.

As she tried to wiggle free from the vines, Raina thought back over the past couple of weeks. Maybe her friends had been right. She had been so stuck on getting the sugar medal, she wasn't seeing straight. Raina knew she should have listened to the fruit flies. If she had listened, maybe she could have saved her candy . . . and not gotten stuck!

"Raina!" Berry called. The Fruit Fairy appeared before her. She was holding a large lollipop umbrella. "Are you hurt?"

"Not hurt," Raina said. "But I'm stuck." She shielded her eyes from the rain so she could see. "What are you doing here?"

"I knew you wouldn't turn around," Berry said. "Even in this awful storm. I came to see if you were all right." She quickly flew up to Raina and untangled her wings from the sticky red stalks. "I'm sorry about what happened

before at Chocolate River," Berry said. "I was just very worried about you."

Raina fluttered her wings and ducked under Berry's umbrella. "I'm sorry too. You were right, you know," she said. "Winning is all I have been thinking about. And I wouldn't listen to anyone." She looked down at her wet dress. "Now all my chances are ruined."

"You don't know that for sure," Berry said. "Come on, let's head back to the forest. Maybe the bushes are fine."

Raina hugged her friend. She was so thankful for her bravery—and her friendship. Berry was a special kind of friend—the *best* kind.

Together, the two fairies flew off into the storm, careful of falling branches and pelting rain.

"What a gooey mess!" Raina cried as she flew over Gummy Forest. The storm had hit the forest hard. Many of the trees were down, and most of the crops looked destroyed. Raina always kept the forest orderly and clean. This was a very sour sight indeed.

As the two fairies landed, the rain began to stop. But the damage was already done.

"Oh no!" Raina cried. Her heart sank as she saw so many of the gummy animals wandering around. They all looked lost. Suddenly her candy for the fair didn't seem as important as helping the animals rebuild their homes.

"Come on, Berry," Raina said, zooming down into the forest. "We have to help."

Berry was right behind her. Her heart ached

when she saw all the sad animals—especially the gummy cubs.

Raina sprang into action. She organized the gummy bears in a line and set up a food station for them. She rounded up the gummy birds, keeping them together. "We'll get this mess sorted out in no time," she told the flock. "Don't worry. We'll get your homes back in order right away."

All the animals listened to Raina as she calmly began the cleanup. She was able to make all the animals feel secure and safe.

Raina bent down to pet a little blue gummy cub. "Don't worry, Blue Belle," she said, smiling. "You'll be just fine."

As Berry watched Raina work, she beamed

with pride. Raina was a talented Candy Fairy and her candy was spectacular, but her true talent was working with the gummy animals. She knew that seeing Gummy Forest in such a mess was upsetting to Raina, but the Gummy Fairy didn't let that show. She was concentrating on helping the animals.

A small gummy bunny hopped up to Raina. He nuzzled his nose into her leg. "I know," Raina said, petting his head. "I promise that you'll be back in your bunny hole by nighttime."

Raina looked around the messy forest and sighed. If only she could find the hole under all the fallen leaves and branches!

Just then Raina looked up to see her friends

Cocoa, Melli, and Dash. Their wings were still wet from the strong rains.

"We're here to help," Cocoa said. "We knew you'd need some extra fairy power."

Raina smiled. She had never been so happy to see her friends! She knew what a great sacrifice they had each made to come to Gummy Forest.

"We knew you'd be upset," Cocoa told her.

"And we wanted to help," Melli said.

"We can get this cleaned up in no time," Dash added.

Raina stared at her friends. They had braved the storm to come help her. She reached out and hugged them. "Thank you," she said. "It's so important that we clean up the branches so that the animals can get back to their homes before nighttime. Will you help?"

"Of course!" Melli exclaimed. "You tell us what to do. Sure as sugar, if we work together, we can clean the forest up by nightfall."

The fairies worked quickly and followed all of Raina's directions. Together, the five friends carried fallen branches, picked up leaves, and uncovered nests. They rebuilt a few homes for the animals and replanted a couple of trees. Very soon the forest was back to normal.

"Here you go," Raina said. She grinned as she placed a young gummy bird back in her nest. "I bet you need a good rest after that storm." She smiled at the bird and then flew back down to the ground.

"Are you ready to head over to Gummy Lake?" Berry asked. Now that all the animals were safe, she knew Raina would be curious about her berry bushes.

"We'll go with you," Melli told her.

The fairies all gathered around Raina.

"Thanks," Raina whispered. She looked around at her friends. "I'm sorry that I've been so stuck on Candy Fair." She wiped a tear from her eye. "I can't believe that it took a big storm to see clearly."

"Don't start crying," Berry said, smiling. "There's been enough water in this forest already today! Besides, don't you want to see what happened to the berry bushes?"

The five fairies flew to Gummy Lake. When

they arrived, Raina saw her berry garden and gasped.

The storm had destroyed the bushes. The branches were broken and the berries were flattened. Just as she had expected, her prized gummy berries were ruined.

CHAPTER

7

A Berry Surprise

Raina sat down at the edge of her berry garden. She peered at the berry bushes. She couldn't believe the sight. Her heart sank as she gazed at the fruit dangling from the branches. Each berry was not only flat, but a swirl of different colors. No longer were there red, blue, yellow, orange, green, and purple berries hanging from the branches. They were all rainbow swirled!

"Oh, sugar sticks!" Raina cried. "Who has ever seen candy quite like this! This is a disaster! I'll have nothing to show at Candy Fair tomorrow."

"The rain must have swirled the colors together," Melli said. She leaned in closer to get

a better view. "You're right. I've never seen any candy like that."

Plucking a berry from the vine, Raina lifted the rainbow-colored candy. She held it up to her friends. "All I could think about were these berries, and now look at them. What kind of Gummy Fairy am I? I should have been home trying to protect the bushes instead of trying to make them even better."

"Oh, Raina," Berry gushed. "You are the kindest Gummy Fairy. Without you, the gummy animals would have been lost and without homes. You were the one who organized the forest clean-up." She took a step closer and plucked the berry from Raina's hand. She held it up to the sun. Carefully, she examined the colorful candy. "Besides, I don't think these berries are ruined," she said.

"What do you think it tastes like?" Dash asked. When she saw the stern looks on her friends' faces, she shrugged. "What? I'm just asking!"

"Dash is right," Berry said. "Maybe the berries taste even better."

Raina shook her head. "Not likely," she said. "Look at them!" She sank down to the soggy, wet ground. "My perfect candy is now a swirl of a mess. I'm sure the flavors are a swirled mess too."

Melli stepped forward. "Don't you remember what Tula said? She said that sometimes the greatest surprises make the sweetest candy."

"She did say that," Cocoa confirmed. "Dash is right. Maybe we should taste the berries."

Berry picked another berry from the branch.

"The candy does look beautiful," she said with a smile. "I have a tie-dye rainbow skirt that looks similar," she said. "Rainbow tie-dye is definitely very fashionable."

Rolling her eyes, Raina sighed. "But rainbow candy?" she said, full of doubt. "Whoever heard of such a gummy thing?"

"That's the point!" Berry replied. "Come on, taste it, Raina. If anyone can make a rainbow taste good, it would be you. You were born on the day the Great Rainbow appeared!"

Berry did have a point. Raina took a bite of the rainbow berry.

"How does it taste?" Cocoa asked, leaning closer to her.

"It tastes . . . ," Raina said as she chewed, "delicious!" A wide smile appeared on her face.

"Lickin' lollipops, I did it!" she cried. Her wings fluttered and she shot straight up in the air. After a quick turn, Raina landed next to the bush and took another candy. She popped the berry in her mouth.

The flavors are a terrific blend, she thought. *Sweet, tangy, and juicy!*

Raina handed a berry to each of her friends.

"It's a rainbow fruit bowl," Melli declared. She licked her fingers and smiled.

"Congratulations," Dash said.

"Gumm-er-ific!" Cocoa added, laughing.

"You see, there is a rainbow after every storm," Berry told her. She gave Raina a tight hug. "And you've just discovered the secret of the rainbow! It's gummy yummy."

"I couldn't have done it without all of you,"

Raina said. She looked around at her friends with a serious expression. "Thank you."

"For what?" Dash asked. She reached out for another rainbow swirl berry.

"For believing in me," Raina said. "And for helping me clear out the forest. You are the sweetest friends a fairy could ever have. Thank you."

They all shared a group hug, and then they picked the berries for Candy Fair. Suddenly Raina had her competitive spirit back. She was ready to go to Candy Fair with her new swirled candy. So what if the candy wasn't perfect—it was perfectly her own. And Raina wanted to share the berries with everyone in Sugar Valley.

CHAPTER

8

Candy Fair

The next morning, the caramel trumpets blew as the royal gates of the castle opened. Candy Fair had officially begun! The Royal Gardens were filled with small white tents, all brimming with candy from Sugar Valley. Rows of tables were set up with Candy Fairies showing their new sweet treats. Some fairies had decorated their booths with candy, and some had fancy stands and signs to showcase their treats. There were old favorites like chocolates, jelly beans, and lollipops. But there were also more elaborate and new candies for the fairies of Sugar Valley to taste.

There was excitement in the air with so many new and delicious treats. Candy Fair was a very special day in the kingdom.

The storm had hit Gummy Forest the hardest, so other candies seemed to have been unharmed by the rain. After the storm the day turned out to be a beautiful and clear spring day.

Cocoa and Melli were at the booth next to Raina's, showing their chocolate-caramel lollipops. The caramel was swirled on a stick like whipped cream on an ice cream sundae. Carefully, Cocoa and Melli had dipped each caramel pop in dark chocolate and dusted the pops with colored sprinkles. Melli had stuck the lollipops into a sugar pinecone, so the pops were displayed beautifully in tiers. Many fairies were lined up to sample the candy.

"Yum!" Dash exclaimed. She reached for another one from the table.

"Hold on," Cocoa said. She stopped Dash's hand before she could touch another pop. "We have to save some for the judges."

"I know," Dash said. She flashed Cocoa a sly smile. "How about just one more?"

Melli slipped Dash another pop. "Last one, okay?" she said. It was hard for her to say no to her friend.

"Thanks, Melli," Dash told her. She took a bite out of the tasty pop. "Sure as sugar, these are the best pops you've ever made."

Raina was happy to see the line of fairies at her booth. Word had spread quickly around the fair that Raina had a new gummy candy. Many of the fairies were curious to see the candy that had survived the rainstorm. And to find out what made Raina's candy so different.

As she handed out her berries to the fairies, Raina heard only good reviews. But Raina knew that the judges were the ones to have the final say on who got the sugar medal. She searched the crowds for Princess Lolli and her advisers.

She was growing a bit concerned. If Princess Lolli didn't come soon, all her berries would be gone! She didn't want to turn away any fairy, but she had to save some for the judges.

When Tula appeared before her, Raina gasped. Seeing one of the judges at her table made her nervous. She knocked over two baskets of her berries! Quickly, she scrambled to pick up the candies. When she stood up, Tula was waiting for her.

"Hello again," Tula said calmly. She pushed her sparkling glasses up on her nose. "Is this the new gummy berry that you told me about at the sign-up?" She held up a berry to take a closer look.

"Not exactly," Raina said. "The candy turned

out a little differently than I had planned."

Tula picked up the rainbow berry and took a bite. "Hmm," she said as she chewed. "How did you get the colors to swirl?"

"The colors just appeared on the berries after the storm—just like a rainbow," Raina said, smiling. "And they are filled with the sweetness of the rain clearing after a storm."

"Very interesting," Tula said. She examined the multicolored berry in her hand. "Different."

"I know that they're not the *perfect* berry," Raina said, hanging her head. Suddenly she felt embarrassed about her less-than-perfect berries. The more Tula examined her candy, the more nervous she became. Slowly, she raised her head. She watched Tula's expression as the Royal Fairy finished eating the candy.

"Ah, but they are *perfectly* sweet," Tula said. She lifted her glasses and peered down at Raina. "Well done, Raina."

"Thank you," Raina said. She thought she was going to burst with pride. "I wouldn't have thought of showing this candy if it weren't for my friends," she added. "They gave me the courage to see that something not perfect might actually be better than planned."

"Yes, friends make life sweeter, that is for sure," Tula said. "And so do acts of kindness." She took off her glasses and looked Raina directly in the eyes. "I heard how you and your friends cleaned up the forest for the gummy animals after the storm yesterday."

"Yes," Raina said. "The forest was quite a mess after all that rain and wind."

"You are a kind and good fairy," Tula said. "And your candy is delicious. Thank you for sharing this candy here today."

Raina couldn't respond. She was too excited. Tula liked her candy! Maybe her dream of getting the sugar medal was going to happen! Raina crossed her fingers for good luck as she watched Tula fly off to the next tent.

"May I try one of your berries?" a small Gummy Fairy asked.

Raina turned her attention back to the line of fairies in front of her table. She smiled at the little fairy and handed her a berry.

"Enjoy," she said.

Holding her hand up to her eyes, Raina shielded the sun from her face and looked around the gardens. Where was Princess Lolli? She hoped the fairy princess and the other two advisers would come soon. The suspense of finding out who would win the sugar medal was growing—and Raina couldn't wait anymore!

Looking up at the sky, she saw the large sun above. Once the sun began to move toward the Frosted Mountains, the judges would have to submit their final decisions. Raina didn't think she could wait till Sun Dip today!

The awards ceremony would start once the sun began to slide behind the mountains. Raina felt as if the day was moving slower than any other day. Everyone in Sugar Valley was eager to hear who would win the sugar medal!

CHAPTER
9

Tasty Tastings

J umping jelly beans!" Berry cried when she saw Raina. She had been flying around the Royal Gardens looking for her friend. There were so many booths set up in the gardens that it took her a long time to find Raina and her booth with the rainbow gummy berries. "Raina, you have the longest line for candy here at the fair." Berry pointed to the line of fairies waiting patiently for their candy.

"I know!" Raina said, working quickly. She was busy handing out her berries, but careful to leave a special basket off to the side. When Princess Lolli finally came, Raina wanted to make sure she had candy for her to sample.

"I'll help you," Berry offered. She landed next to Raina and started to hand out the rainbow candies. "Try a yummy gummy berry!" she called out.

Raina smiled. Berry's enthusiasm was making everyone excited about the new candy. She was thrilled that Berry had come to the fair.

"Thank you for coming today," Raina told her.

"I wouldn't have missed it!" she cried. "Just because I didn't want to show my own candy didn't mean I wouldn't be here for you."

Raina gave Berry a tight hug. "Thank you."

As she pulled away from her friend, she noticed a little Chocolate Fairy staring at Berry's necklace.

"I love your necklace," the little fairy said to Berry.

Blushing, Berry smiled. "Thanks," she said. "I made it out of fresh fruit chews."

"Sugar snaps," the fairy cheered. "I'd love one. Could you make one for me?"

"Sure," Berry replied, grinning.

"I told you other fairies would love the jewelry!" Raina said, giving Berry a nudge.

"You might be on to something," Berry agreed. "I have gotten a few comments on the necklace today." She put her arm around Raina. "But today is about sweet candy—and the sugar medal. Has Princess Lolli been here yet?"

"No," Raina said, shaking her head. She was beginning to wonder if the princess would ever come sample her candy. She didn't have time to fret, though. There were too many fairies wanting to try her rainbow candies. As she spoke, she continued to pass out her yummy gummy berries. All the fairies seemed to be enjoying the treat, and Raina was so pleased.

"What if I run out before Princess Lolli gets here?" Raina whispered to Berry.

At that very moment Princess Lolli stepped

up to Raina's table. With her were two Royal Fairies. They were ready to judge her candy!

"What do we have here?" the fairy princess asked. She gave Raina a warm smile. Her beautiful long pink dress flowed out behind her. "These look gorgeous. May I have one, please?"

"Oh, yes, of course!" Raina exclaimed. She handed a rainbow berry to the fairy princess.

Holding her breath, Raina tried to wait patiently as Princess Lolli tasted her candy. The princess fixed her candy tiara on top of her long strawberry-blond hair.

"Very good, Raina," she declared. "This year it seems there are so many new candies. I think we have some tough decisions to make." The princess turned to her two advisers and handed them each a berry.

Raina stood still as a sugar cube. She wasn't sure what to say to the princess!

"We will be announcing the awards soon," Princess Lolli said. "Raina, these berries were a very sweet treat."

As the fairy princess spoke, the two advisers scribbled notes on a large parchment scroll.

Raina was so curious about what the two advisers wrote! She had to wonder if they liked the different berries, and if they thought they were worthy of the sugar medal.

"Everyone has done a great job!" the princess exclaimed. "Even with the terrible storm. This will be a very difficult decision for us to make. Thank you, Raina, and good luck!"

The fairy princess flew off to another tent with her two advisers by her side. She still

had more tastings to do before Sun Dip.

Raina sighed. She leaned on the table in front of her.

"Don't worry," Berry whispered. She stood close to her friend and squeezed her shoulder. "I think Princess Lolli liked the berry very much."

"Do you really think so?" Raina asked. "Maybe she is saying those nice things to all the fairies who made candy."

"I don't think so," Berry said, shaking her head.

Raina wasn't sure what Princess Lolli was thinking. She was only sure that she would find waiting for the awards ceremony very difficult!

CHAPTER 10

The Sweetest Award

Finally the caramel horns blew again, announcing that the awards ceremony would begin shortly. All the fairies moved to the center of the gardens, where a stage was set up. Princess Lolli, Tula, and three other Royal Fairies were sitting on royal chairs on the stage. Princess Lolli was in the middle, sitting in her candy throne bedazzled with crystal candy jewels.

"Welcome to Candy Fair!" Princess Lolli said to the large crowd of fairies. "This year was an extraordinarily sweet year. A big fairy thank-you to all the fairies who prepared so many candy treats." She turned to smile at the advisers behind her. "We had a very difficult decision to make. There were many, many worthy candies this year."

Raina held Berry's hand. Standing around them were Melli, Cocoa, and Dash. At that moment Raina was happy to have her friends near. Without them, this moment would not have been as special.

Dash moaned and rubbed her belly. "I think I ate too much candy today," she said. "Princess Lolli is right. Everything was so yummy. I couldn't stop myself!"

"That's why Candy Fair is every four years, not every year," Berry said with a grin.

"And now for the moment we've all been waiting for," Princess Lolli said. She looked around at the crowd, smiling. "I am pleased to present this year's sugar medal to . . ."

Everyone was quiet. Raina closed her eyes and squeezed Berry's and Melli's hands.

"The winner of the sugar medal is," Princess Lolli announced, "Miro the Gummy Fairy for her beautiful and tasty gummy flowers!"

A roar of applause erupted. Raina turned to see Miro. She was grinning as she flew up to the stage to get her medal.

Though Raina felt disappointed, she was proud of Miro. The young fairy had listened to the fruit flies' warnings and taken good care of her crops during the storm. She deserved praise for her fine gummy candy. Raina was very happy that for the first time ever a Gummy Fairy had won the medal.

She felt Berry squeeze her hand. She squeezed Berry's hand back, thankful again that her friends were by her side.

"And finally," Princess Lolli said. She put her hands up to quiet the crowd. "There is one more award this year."

A hush came over the crowd of fairies.

"It is not often that this award is given," Princess Lolli said. "And I am especially proud to award this to a very special fairy."

"What is this about?" Raina whispered to Berry. She had no idea what the princess was talking about. The sugar medal was the first prize. What other award could there be? She had never read about another award in any of her books. Sure, there were honorable mentions, but another award?

Berry shrugged and looked back to the fairy princess.

Everyone was eager to hear what the princess had to say.

"I would like to award the great honor of the pink candy heart to Raina the Gummy Fairy," Princess Lolli proclaimed. "The special pink candy heart is for her dedication to the animals in Gummy Forest. On behalf of the entire Candy Kingdom, and all of Sugar Valley," the princess said, "we thank you for your hard work. The animals would not have had a place to stay after the storm if it hadn't been for your quick thinking and dedication."

All the fairies in the Royal Gardens cheered wildly. The Gummy Fairies were the loudest. Raina gave a small wave, blushing. She didn't win the sugar medal, but the pink candy heart was a thrilling surprise. As Princess Lolli said, the pink candy heart was not given often, and it was a true treasure.

She looked over and saw Tula smiling at her.

"This will go down in the books as a very special day for all the Gummy Fairies," Princess Lolli continued. "And for all Candy Fairies everywhere."

"Well, go get your award," Berry said, nudging Raina toward the stage.

Raina looked at her friends. "You all need to come with me. We all worked together that day, and you deserve the honor too."

The five fairies held hands and flew up to the stage. Princess Lolli pinned the sugar crystal pink heart on Raina's dress.

"I'm very proud of you," the fairy princess told her. "And those rainbow gummy berries were delicious!" She leaned in closer. "Do you think we can grow more of them?"

"Sure as sugar!" Raina blurted out.

"I'm glad," Princess Lolli said. "Thank you, Raina."

Raina took in all the praise, and then looked up at the princess. "Thank you, Princess Lolli," Raina said. Then she grabbed her friends and brought them onstage with her. "But I wouldn't

have been able to do anything without my friends. They were a great help. I want to share this award with them."

The loud cheers from the Royal Gardens swept up high into the Frosted Mountains. Raina beamed with pride.

"You look great with that candy heart," Berry

said, smiling at her friend. "Well deserved!"

"And it's so sparkly and shiny!" Dash remarked.

"It is special," Melli said.

"Congratulations!" Cocoa added.

"Thank you," Raina said. She hugged her friends. "This was a sweet surprise. And I'll treasure this award forever . . . just like I treasure all of you!"

Raina's candy hadn't turned out as she planned, and Candy Fair did not go as expected. But she couldn't have been happier. Indeed, the sweetest events are not always the ones planned. And they are made even sweeter when surrounded by good, true friends.

Caramel Moon

For Bethany Buck,

who was born under a Caramel Moon!

Contents

CHAPTER 1	Golden News	229
CHAPTER 2	Trouble in the Fields	240
CHAPTER 3	Candy Clues	250
CHAPTER 4	Sweet Moonlight	262
CHAPTER 5	Super-Spies	273
CHAPTER 6	Ghoulish Plans	284
CHAPTER 7	Ghost Lessons	295
CHAPTER 8	Clean-up Crew	305
CHAPTER 9	Sugar Dust	316
CHAPTER 10	Under the Caramel Moon	325

1

Golden News

The caramel stalks on the hill glowed golden in the late afternoon sun. Melli, a Caramel Fairy, took a deep breath. She smelled the sweet, sugary scent of fresh caramel. Sitting on a branch of a chocolate oak, she gave a heavy sigh. It was nice to relax after a day's work in the fields.

From the tree she could see out to Caramel

Hills and Candy Corn Fields. This was one of her favorite spots in Sugar Valley. A gentle breeze blew her short, dark hair. The cool air reminded her that the weather was turning colder. While she was sorry that the long, sunny days of summer were over, Melli loved the change of season.

Autumn was the busiest time of year for the Caramel Fairies. Many of their candies were grown and harvested in the autumn months. And Melli's favorite was candy corn. Not only did she love the sweet treat, she loved the Caramel Moon Festival, too.

This event, the best event of the fall, was held during the evening of the full moon in the tenth month of the year. Princess Lolli, the ruling fairy princess of Candy Kingdom, officially named that moon Caramel Moon. The candy corn was at the peak of perfection at that time, and all the candy crops needed to be picked when they were ripe, so all the fairies in Sugar Valley came to help. The festival was a giant party with lots of candy corn, music, and dancing.

"Hi, Melli!" Cara called out. Cara was Melli's little sister. She flew up and sat on the branch beside Melli.

"Hey, Cara," Melli said. "How'd you find me?"

"I knew you'd be here," Cara told her. "It's almost Sun Dip and you always wait for Cocoa here."

Melli laughed. Her little sister was right. The chocolate oak at the bottom of Caramel Hill was at the edge of Chocolate Woods. The old tree was the perfect meeting spot for her and her best friend, Cocoa the Chocolate Fairy. They always flew together to see their friends at the end of the day when the sun dipped below the Frosted Mountains. Sun Dip was a time for meeting friends and sharing news of the day.

"I just heard some golden news," Cara went on. A smile spread across her face. "You'll never guess who is playing at the Caramel Moon Festival this year!" Her lavender wings fluttered so fast that she flew up off the branch.

"You found out who is playing?" Melli asked. Her dark eyes sparkled with excitement.

All year long, fairies tried to guess who would play the music at the late-night celebration. After the candy corn was picked, all the fairies celebrated by the light of the moon. Good music was a key ingredient to making the party a success.

Since this year Melli was old enough to have planted the seeds in the fields, she was even more excited about the festival.

Cara grinned at Melli. She usually didn't hear juicy information before her older sister. She wanted to savor the sweet moment of knowing something before Melli.

"Come on," Melli urged. "Please tell me! I want to know!" She grabbed Cara's hand.

"Well, it's your favorite band," Cara said. She looked as if she would burst with excitement.

Melli's mouth fell open. "The Sugar Pops are coming here?" Her purple wings began to flutter, and her heart began to beat faster. "Are you sure?"

"Sure as sugar," Cara said. "I was at Candy Castle to make a delivery and I heard the Royal Fairies talking about the Caramel Moon Festival. The Sugar Pops are really coming!"

The Sugar Pops were the most popular band in the entire kingdom. Their music was fun to dance to, and Melli knew every single song by heart. She also knew everything about Chip, Char, and Carob Pop. The three Pop brothers sang *and* played instruments. They had the sweetest songs.

"Hot caramel!" Melli exclaimed. "Wait until I tell everyone at Sun Dip!" She reached out and hugged her sister. "Thanks for telling me, Cara. This is fantastic news." Her mind was racing. "If they sing 'Yum Pop,' I will melt!"

Cara nodded. "Oh, they have to play that

song!" she exclaimed. "It's their best one." She smiled.

Melli looked toward Chocolate Woods. She kept an eye out for Cocoa. Cocoa loved the Sugar Pops too. Actually, all her friends did. And this year they would be able to stay and help harvest the crops, which meant they'd also get to see the Sugar Pops perform.

"What about me? Do you think I can watch the Sugar Pops?" Cara asked.

"I'll see if I can get you permission," Melli said. She leaned in closer to Cara and put her arm around her. She didn't want to see her sister so sad. "Maybe you can come for one or two songs."

"Thanks, Melli," Cara said. Her wings perked up a little at the possibility of seeing the band play.

Just at that moment, Cocoa flew up to the chocolate oak. "Hello, fairies!" she called out. "What's new and delicious?"

Melli and Cara both grinned.

"What?" Cocoa asked. She looked at the two sisters. "What are you up to?"

Melli's wings flapped and she floated off the branch. She couldn't contain her excitement! "Cara found out that the Sugar Pops are playing at the Caramel Moon Festival!" she burst out.

Cocoa clapped her hands. *Choc-o-rific!* she shouted. "That is the sweetest news I've heard all day!" She sat down on one of the chocolate oak's branches. "Wait until the others hear about this. And this year we'll get to stay the whole night!"

Melli nudged Cocoa. She knew that Cara was feeling sad about not being old enough to

stay for the night concert. "We're going to see if Cara can come for at least one song," she told Cocoa.

"'Yum Pop', I hope," Cara said. She held up crossed fingers.

Melli and Cocoa laughed.

"Come on," Cocoa said. "Let's head over to Sun Dip and tell the others."

"I want to go check on the candy corn crops before Sun Dip," Melli said. "All the Caramel Fairies were working near Caramel Hills today. I haven't been since yesterday. I'll meet you at Red Licorice Lake."

Melli gave quick hugs to Cara and Cocoa.

"I'll see you later," Cara called as she flew back home to Caramel Hills.

"See you soon, Cara," Cocoa said. "And, Melli, bring some of your caramel!"

"Of course!" Melli called. She still had a smile on her face as she flew toward the fields.

The Caramel Moon Festival was bound to be the most extraordinary event of the year!

2

Trouble in the Fields

Melli found herself alone in Candy Corn Fields. The early evening chill felt refreshing, and the crisp smell of the crops meant that harvest time was nearing.

As she flew through the fields, she hummed a Sugar Pops song. She imagined how fun it would be to dance to their music at midnight after all the crops were picked. There would be a stage set up at the north side of the fields. Large barrels of candy corn would line the stage, and Princess Lolli would welcome all the Candy Fairies. She was a fair and true ruler, who took good care of all the fairies in Sugar Valley. And she was also a huge fan of the Sugar Pops!

Melli wondered if she would get to meet the Pop boys. She had to at least get their autographs! She fluttered her wings just thinking of the three sweet singers.

Landing in the green fields, Melli looked around. Her wings drooped as she spun in a circle. It wasn't the color of the stalks or the shapes of the hanging candy corn that concerned her. But something was wrong. Very wrong.

She flapped her wings and flew up and down the rows. Her wings beat faster as she looked around. All the stalks were much shorter than they had been the day before. The stalks were supposed to grow taller, with candy corn dripping from the wide leaves. But at that moment it seemed to Melli that the stalks had shrunk.

How can this be? she thought. *What happened? I was just here yesterday.*

As Melli flew up and down the rows of candy corn stalks, she didn't notice the darkening sky. The sun had just slipped down past the Frosted Mountains when she heard Cocoa's voice.

"Melli!" Cocoa cried. She waved her hands, trying to get her friend's attention.

"Over here," Melli answered. She didn't look up from the stalk she was examining.

"What's the matter? You missed Sun Dip!" Cocoa said as she flew up to Melli. "Everyone was so worried."

"Something is not right here," Melli blurted out. She pointed to the stalks around them.

Melli slowly walked a few steps. She leaned in close to the stalks. The white, yellow, and orange candy corn looked all right, but something seemed off to her. "These stalks were higher yesterday," she explained to Cocoa. She flapped her wings and took off down the row.

"What do you mean?" Cocoa asked. She took flight and followed her friend. "Everything looks fine."

As Cocoa flew down the long rows, the green leaves of the stalks tickled her arms. She saw that all the stalks were filled with candy corn. "The candy corn looks delicious," she said. "Especially the ones on the far end of the field."

"You mean the ones with the chocolate tips?" Melli asked. She knew that Cocoa preferred the ones with a touch of chocolate.

"Actually," Cocoa said, "all these look ready for harvesting." She smelled the sweet scent of ripe candy corn. "This all looks good to me."

"I'm telling you, something is wrong," Melli replied. Her wings fluttered quickly as she flew down to examine another stalk. She shook her head sadly. "Caramel Moon is two days from now. What happens if the candy corn doesn't ripen in time? Or worse, if the candy corn shrinks and disappears!"

Cocoa gasped. There had never been a year without candy corn. She wasn't sure what all the fairies would do without the special autumn treat.

"How can we have a Caramel Moon Festival without candy corn?" Melli cried out.

Cocoa put her arm around her friend. "Don't be silly," she said. "The corn is always ready on the night of Caramel Moon. You worry too much." She spun around and looked at the rows of green stalks. "The fields are full, and the candy corn looks ready to harvest!" She saw that Melli was still concerned. "Has Princess Lolli been here yet? Maybe she can help."

"She hasn't been here yet," Melli said. "She said she'll be by soon to check on the crops." Melli stepped on a mound of soft brown sugar. "I don't really want her to see the fields looking

like this!" Staring down at the ground, she mumbled, "What if I did something wrong?"

"What are you talking about?" Cocoa asked. "I think you are just nervous. All this talk about the Sugar Pops coming has distracted you!"

"No," Melli said. She searched the fields for a clue. "This is strange."

"I don't know," Cocoa told her. "Maybe you just have the sugar jitters for the big day."

Melli ducked low and peered under one of the stalks. "Look!" she cried, pointing. "There's a mound of brown sugar here," she said. "And fallen candy corn on the ground over there." She crawled under a stalk and followed the trail of clues.

Cocoa came with her. Maybe Melli was right. Normally, the fields didn't look like someone—

or something—had been pulling corn off the stalks.

"The whole north part of the field is ruined!" Melli exclaimed. "Someone has been messing with the candy corn crops. And we have to find out who!"

Cocoa bent down and picked up a mashed candy corn. "Look at this," she said. "You're right, Melli. Candy corn doesn't get mashed by itself."

Melli's eyes widened. "Do you think someone is trying to ruin the Caramel Moon Festival?" she asked.

"I don't know," Cocoa admitted. "But sure as sugar, we need to find out!"

CHAPTER

3

Candy Clues

As Melli and Cocoa picked up the fallen stalks and candy corn, their friends arrived at Candy Corn Fields.

"What's going on?" Raina asked. The Gummy Fairy looked worried as she saw her friends scurrying around the fields.

Dash, a Mint Fairy, flew above them. "Are

you picking the candy before Caramel Moon?"

"Of course they aren't," Berry said. The beautiful Fruit Fairy landed on the ground and leaned over to smell the candy corn. "Everyone knows that the candy isn't picked until midnight of the Caramel Moon."

"Someone has been messing with the crops," Melli blurted out.

"Are you sure?" Berry asked. She looked around the dark fields. "What makes you think that?"

Melli pointed to the basket of smashed candy corn and broken stalks that she and Cocoa had collected. "See?" she said. "The north side of the field was a mess. I think someone was trying to take all the candy corn."

"No one has ever stolen candy corn from the

fields," Raina said, shaking her head. Raina knew the whole history of the Candy Fairies and Candy Kingdom. She loved to read and had memorized the Fairy Code Book. "I've never heard of such a story about Candy Corn Fields."

"There's a first time for everything," Dash said as she landed on top of one of the candy corn stalks.

"Dash!" Berry scolded. She saw Melli's worried expression. She didn't want to send Melli into a sugar fit. She already looked like she was ready to have a meltdown.

"Maybe one of the other Caramel Fairies was trying to get the fields ready?" Raina offered.

"No Caramel Fairy would pick the candy before Caramel Moon," Melli said. "The Caramel Fairies were working in the south part of the fields yesterday. This must have happened overnight and no one checked on this side today." She examined the stalk next to her. "It's almost as if someone was trying to pull down the stalks." She pointed to the short stalk in front of her.

"Remember those chocolate bugs that ate away at the trees in Chocolate Woods last year?" Cocoa asked. "Maybe it's some kind of candy field bug?"

Raina shook her head. "They wouldn't be strong enough," she said. "These stalks are thick and very sturdy." She reached over and gave the green stalk a tug. "And there haven't been any great storms like the one that hit Gummy Forest in the spring."

"My guess is Mogu," Berry said. She folded

her arms across her chest. "That mischievous troll is always out to steal Candy Fairy treats."

"Maybe," Cocoa said, nodding. A shiver spread to the tip of her wings as she remembered her journey to Black Licorice Swamp with Princess Lolli. When Cocoa's chocolate eggs were missing, she and the fairy princess journeyed to Mogu's cave to get them back. It was a dangerous trek, and Cocoa didn't want to think about going back to that black swamp again.

"I'm thinking it was the Chuchies," Melli said, sitting down on the ground. She leaned against one of the stalks. "You see the ground here? There weren't mounds of brown sugar here yesterday. And Chuchies are short, so it makes sense that they'd try to pull the stalks."

"And Chuchies always leave a mess behind," Berry said, agreeing with Melli.

"Those furry little creatures could have tramped through here last night," Raina said, looking around. "They are so sneaky, they could have come in without anyone seeing them."

"But you know those Chuchies don't act alone," Cocoa added.

"Mogu," Berry said again. "I just know he is behind this."

Melli put her head in her hands. "So what do we do about it?"

"First we need to make sure it really was the Chuchies," Raina said. "Maybe it was someone else?"

The fairy friends were silent as they all considered who might have been responsible.

"What if all the candy is gone tomorrow?" Dash said in a panic.

"Then the Sugar Pops probably won't come," Melli said sadly.

"The Sugar Pops?" Berry, Raina, and Dash all said at the same time.

Melli had been so happy to tell her friends about the Sugar Pops coming, but now the news wasn't as exciting. If there were no crops, there wouldn't be a big celebration.

"Cara overheard the Royal Fairies talking at Candy Castle about them coming to perform," Cocoa explained.

"I was so excited to see them," Melli said sadly. "But who knows if they will come if there's no festival."

"Holy peppermint!" Dash exclaimed. "You

mean Chip, Char, and Carob are going to be here? Right here?" She flew straight up in the air.

Cocoa nodded. "That was the plan," she explained.

"We definitely need to solve this candy corn mystery," Berry said.

"You can bet your sugar fruit chews," Cocoa said. "This was the first year we were going to get to stay till midnight!"

"And meet the Sugar Pops," Dash added with a dreamy look in her eye.

"Well, at least there are a few candy clues," Berry noted. "Do you think we can figure this out?"

"We can solve this mystery," Melli said, standing up. "We have to!"

Raina paced up and down. She tapped her

finger on her chin as she thought out loud. "There's a story in the Fairy Code Book about Lupa the Sugar Fairy," she began. "She was sure that a troll was stealing her sugar fruit chews and wanted to protect her candy."

"Oh, I know that story!" Berry exclaimed. "Lupa caught the troll in the middle of the night and sent him back over the Frosted Mountains. She was very brave."

Melli walked over to Raina. "How did she do that?" she asked.

"Well," Raina said, "the story goes that she built a spy tower so that she could watch the fields at night and spot the troll. She used sticky sugar syrup in a hidden trap to slow the troll down. And she captured him!"

"Wow!" Dash cried. *So mint.*

The more Melli thought about the crops and the festival, the braver she felt. She had to be as clever as Lupa had been. She knew she had to do something to make sure that the Caramel Moon Festival happened this year.

"I have a plan," she declared. "Let's meet back here right before Sun Dip tomorrow. We're going to build a tower just like Lupa. I'm sure whoever did this will be back for more tonight. And we'll be waiting."

Melli's friends all stared at her. The Caramel Fairy seemed very sure of herself. But would they be successful like Lupa had been? How would they stop whoever—or whatever—was trying to ruin Caramel Moon?

4

Sweet Moonlight

The sun was just about to slip down below the tops of the Frosted Mountains. Melli stood with her four friends at the edge of Candy Corn Fields. A cool breeze blew their wings, but they were all still. They were anxious to hear Melli's plan for building the spy tower.

"We'll build the tower here," Melli said. She

pointed to a clearing in Lollipop Landing. "We'll be able to see all the fields if we make the tower high enough."

Dash opened her bag. "I brought peppermint sticks that glow in the dark," she said. "I thought that would help."

"And I brought some gummy lanterns," Raina said. She held up two lanterns to show her friends. One lantern glowed a deep red light, and the other orange.

Melli smiled. "Thanks," she said.

Cocoa took a box out of her bag. "And I brought a telescope," she said. "It's made out of the finest chocolate with a special sugar glass lens." She held it up to her eye. "Perfect for spying," she added.

"That looks like the kind of telescope that Lupa used," Raina said, taking a closer look.

"Come on," Melli told them. "There isn't much daylight left, and we've got work to do."

"Where's Berry?" Dash asked, looking around.

Raina shrugged. "She said that she had to get something."

"It's not like we're meeting the Sugar Pops tonight," Cocoa said, joking. "But she probably still wanted to change into some special spy outfit for the spying occasion."

Just then Berry came flying up to the group. "I'm here!" she called. "And I have some sticky fruit syrup for the traps," she said. She showed her friends a large bottle of gooey red syrup. "It's what Lupa used, so I thought it would help."

"Thanks, Berry," Melli told her. "I set some traps down in the fields, and the sticky syrup will be perfect."

"But you know," Raina said, "Chuchies can sniff those traps out. They can pick up scents from miles away."

Melli nodded. "I know," she said, "but it's worth a try. If the thieves aren't the Chuchies, then maybe the traps will stop them."

Quickly the five friends worked together to build a spy tower. Raina and Berry flew in tall lollipop sticks, and Dash and Cocoa lifted rolls of fruit leather to make the floor. Melli tied the lollipop sticks together with licorice vines and secured the tall tower. Then the fairies set up the lanterns and peppermint sticks at the top.

By the time they finished with the tower, the sky was getting dark. There was a chill in the air and Melli shivered.

"Okay, so we'll take turns using Cocoa's telescope," she said. "And we'll check on the traps every hour."

"When we catch the candy corn thieves," Cocoa said, "we'll be the heroes of Caramel Moon!"

"I hope you're right," Melli told her. She picked up the telescope and peered through the lens. "So far the fields are quiet."

Berry wrapped herself in a white shawl. "It's cold out tonight!" she exclaimed.

"Is that new?" Dash asked, admiring Berry's shawl.

"Yes," Berry said proudly. "It's made from

the finest white cotton candy and finished with a raw sugar fringe."

"Wow," Dash said, admiring the details.

"It's warm, too," Berry told her. "Do you want to share it with me?"

Dash shook her head. "No, I like this cold weather," she answered. "It makes me feel like winter is almost here."

"Don't say that!" Raina cried. "We haven't even celebrated Caramel Moon. Winter is a long time away."

"It can't come soon enough," Dash replied. "I want to hit the slopes with my new sled."

Dash lived for the winter, when she could sled. Even though she was the smallest fairy in Sugar Valley, she was a champion on the slopes.

The five friends huddled together as they

watched the fields from the high tower.

Melli stood up and walked to the edge of the tower. She didn't see anything unusual. The Candy Corn stalks all stood upright, swaying in the night breeze. She sighed heavily. "What will we do if we don't see anything?" she asked.

"We just have to be patient," Raina advised. "Lupa had to sit in her tower for a week before she saw anything."

"Raina!" Melli cried out. "We don't have a week! Caramel Moon is tomorrow night!"

The evening wind gently shook the tower.

"It's spooky here," Dash said.

"And dark," Cocoa added. "It's a good thing the moon is almost full so we can keep watch."

"But it is a little scary," Berry said, pulling her knees up to her chest.

"I'll crack another peppermint stick," Dash told them. A little spark from the stick lit up the tower.

Raina yawned. "I'm so sleepy," she said. "I had to clean up Gummy Forest today. Those gummy cubs made a huge mess playing in the woods."

"Maybe we should take turns keeping watch over the fields," Cocoa suggested.

Melli pressed the telescope to her eye. "I'll take the first turn," she said. "I am too nervous to sleep. If something is going to happen, I want to be ready."

"Well, wake us up if you see something," Berry said, lying down. Her eyes were heavy and she longed to get a little rest.

"I'll stay up with you," Cocoa told Melli. "Don't worry," she whispered, "I'm sure we'll see something soon."

Melli hoped Cocoa was right. She kept her eyes on the fields below, searching for any sign. But so far only the winds were making the stalks sway in the moonlight.

CHAPTER
5

Super-Spies

The round moon rose high in the sky. Melli was thankful for the soft white moonlight. She kept a careful watch on the fields as her friends slept.

Melli spread Berry's soft white shawl over the sleeping fairies. They were all huddled together on the floor of the tower. Even Cocoa had drifted off to sleep. But Melli was wide awake. She knew that whoever—or whatever—was harming the crops would strike soon. And she wanted to be ready.

She picked up the chocolate telescope and gazed through the lens. Zooming in on the fields below, she looked for any sign of trouble. But the fields were quiet. She would just have to wait.

Melli turned back to her sleeping friends. She was so thankful that they were with her on this spying mission.

Next to Raina, Melli saw the book with the Lupa the Sugar Fairy story. She picked it up and searched for the tale about Lupa and the mischievous troll. As she read about Lupa's adventures, she grew more and more impatient waiting for something to happen in the fields.

Once again she stood up and looked through the telescope.

"Hot caramel!" she cried.

Cocoa woke with a start. "What? What happened?" she said, jumping up.

Melli gave Cocoa the telescope and pointed to the north side of the field.

"Over there!" she said. "I knew it! I knew those little furry Chuchies were the cause of all this mess."

"Look at them," Cocoa said. She watched the Chuchies scurry around on their thin, short legs. "They are so sneaky. Look how they are coming up from underneath the stalks."

"That's why the stalks seem shorter!" Melli declared. "The Chuchies have been digging tunnels in the field to pull the stalks down! They couldn't reach the candy unless they pulled the stalks lower."

"Chocolate sprinkles!" Cocoa exclaimed. "You're right!"

"I'm going to go see exactly what they are doing," Melli said bravely.

Cocoa put the telescope down. "Then I'm going with you." She grabbed Melli's hand. "You shouldn't go alone."

Together, the two fairies flew down into Candy Corn Fields. Melli tried not to think about the long shadows in the field or the howling wind. She flew quickly and landed behind a large candy corn stalk. Without saying a word, she pointed to a mound of brown sugar. Then she and Cocoa hid as a couple of Chuchies shuffled by.

"Meeee, meeeee!" squealed one of the Chuchies. With a little jump, the furry creature grabbed a bunch of candy corn. Then it jumped over the sticky syrup trap.

Another Chuchie popped up from the underground tunnel. It shook off the brown sugar dirt from its pom-pom-shaped body. "Meeee Meeeee!" it sang out. The Chuchie held up a basket and plunked in several pieces of candy corn.

Melli wanted to run out from her hiding space and grab the candy back. She saw about five more Chuchies crawl out of the tunnel with baskets. If she and her friends didn't act soon, all the candy corn would be gone by the time the sun rose. Melli knew that in order to save the crops, she had to be smart. The Chuchies

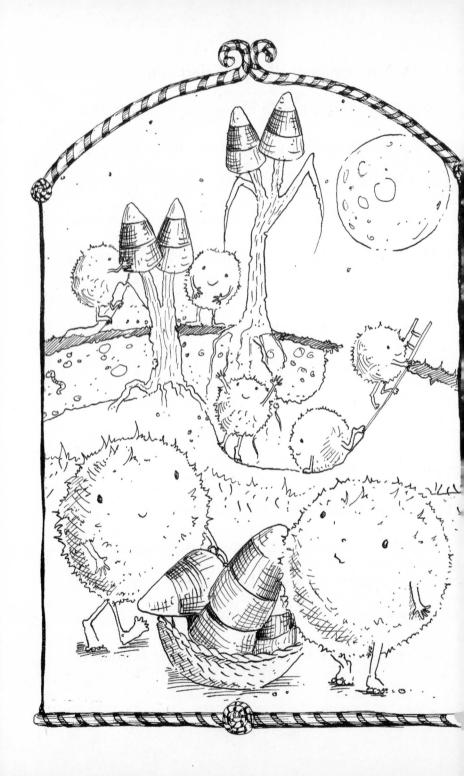

weren't the cleverest creatures, but they were determined . . . especially about stealing candy.

Waving her hand, she motioned for Cocoa to fly back to the tower, where they could talk.

When they were away from the field, Melli let out a sigh. "How can we stop them? Those mischievous Chuchies can't just take our candy."

Raina stretched and yawned. "Did you see something?" she asked, half asleep. "What's going on?"

As Raina sat up, Berry and Dash opened their eyes. Melli sat down on the floor next to her friends. "Cocoa and I saw the Chuchies taking the candy corn," she told them. "They dug tunnels under the fields."

"We have to stop them!" Dash exclaimed.

"But how?" Raina asked. "Chuchies are quick, and strong."

"But not always smart," Berry pointed out.

Melli gazed toward the field. "We need a plan," she said. She bent down and picked up Raina's book.

"What would Lupa do?" Dash asked. "She caught the troll. She knew what she was doing."

"She was one of the bravest Candy Fairies ever," Raina said. "She defeated lots of trolls and dragons."

Berry stood up. "We can be just as clever," she said. "No way are those little Chuchies going to get away with stealing candy corn . . . or ruining the Caramel Moon Festival."

"Or spoiling our chance to meet the Sugar Pops," Cocoa chimed in.

Hugging the book to her chest, Melli wished she could be as brave and as clever as Lupa had been. She stared at the Chuchies scurrying around in the moonlit field. "We have to do something to make them stop."

Raina stood up and put her arm around Melli. "There's still time," she said calmly.

"There's a ton of candy corn this year," Cocoa added. "There will be plenty for the celebration."

Berry shook her head. "But Melli's right. We need a plan. We need a way to stop the Chuchies. If we don't, we can say good-bye to the Sugar Pops."

"Don't be so sour," Raina said. "We can come up with a plan."

"But we better act fast," Melli said, biting her

nails. "The Chuchies have almost cleared the north part of the field."

She wanted to believe that she and her friends could stop what was going on . . . the only question was how!

CHAPTER

6

Ghoulish Plans

As Melli and her friends huddled together in the tower, a strong wind blew through the fields. The wind picked up Berry's white shawl and blew it off the tower into the dark night.

"Oh no!" Berry cried. She leaned over the side of the tower. "That's my new shawl!" She squinted into the darkness. "Where did it go?"

Dash got up and stood next to Berry. Leaning over the railing, she searched down below.

"We'll find it," Raina said gently. "Don't worry."

"I see the shawl," Dash said. She pointed to the left of the tower. "There it is!"

"Oh, thank you, Dash," Berry gushed, giving her tiny friend a tight squeeze.

"It looks like a ghost, doesn't it?" Cocoa said, looking down at the shawl.

Raina shivered. "Don't talk about ghosts," she said. "It's creepy enough out here in the moonlight and howling winds."

Dash put her hands on her hips. "Oh, come on," she said. "Are you really scared?"

Melli's eyes grew wide. "That's it!" she exclaimed. "Raina, you're brilliant!"

Berry, Raina, Dash, and Cocoa all shared confused looks.

"That's the perfect way to stop the Chuchies," Melli declared, grinning.

"What are you talking about?" Cocoa asked. "Did I just miss something?"

Melli couldn't help smiling. She knew that her plan was going to work. Swooping down to the ground, she picked up Berry's shawl and brought it back up to the tower. She put the shawl over her head and reached her hands out to the sides.

"Put the candy corn down!" she said in the spookiest voice she could.

Cocoa laughed out loud.

But Dash clapped. "Scare the Chuchies!" she said. She flapped her wings and flew up in the air. "Oh, that is pure sugar!"

"Do you think that will work?" Berry asked. She took the shawl off Melli's head and hugged it close. "This is made from the finest sugar, you know."

Cocoa rolled her eyes. "Yes, we know," she said.

"It's a good idea," Raina told Melli. "Chuchies are known to react out of fear." She opened her Fairy Code Book and flipped through the pages. Then she ran her finger down the page until she found what she was looking for at the bottom. "'Chuchies react quickly to things that confuse or scare them,'" she read.

"If it's written in the Fairy Code Book, then it must be true!" Melli said happily.

Raina grinned, but Berry shook her head.

"Come on," Berry said. "How are you going to get those Chuchies to believe that my shawl is a ghost?"

Cocoa saw Melli starting to panic.

"We'll figure out a way," Cocoa said. "We can do it!"

Melli was thankful for Cocoa's enthusiasm. She held up a large round lollipop. "We can drape the shawl over this," she explained. "And then we can put the stick in the ground." She tilted her head and examined the ghost. "Our ghost is going to need some kind of eerie glow."

"Use one of my peppermint sticks," Dash suggested. She flew closer to Melli and cracked open one of her glow-in-the-dark candies. Sprinkling the peppermint candy around the inside of the shawl made their ghost start to glow.

"Hey, now it's starting to look like the Ghost of Candy Corn Fields!" Cocoa cheered.

Raina looked up from her book. "The ghost will need a voice," she said.

"I know!" Cocoa cried. "Wait one second!" She flew off the tower and out into the darkness. In a flash she was back with a chocolate sugar cone. She broke off the pointy end. "Here, talk into this," she told Melli. "This cone from Chocolate Woods will make you sound bigger and scarier."

"Thanks, Cocoa," Melli said, taking the cone. She did as Cocoa had told her and spoke into the long sugar cone.

"Put down the candy corn!" Melli bellowed.

"It still sounds like you," Berry said. She crossed her arms over her chest.

"Berry!" Cocoa cried. "Maybe your sugar clips are in too tight." She pointed to the sugarcoated fruit chews in Berry's hair.

Berry ignored Cocoa. Tapping her finger on her chin, Berry thought for a moment. "Hold on," she said. "I have an idea." She dove off the top of the tower again. "I'll be right back."

"What is she up to?" Melli asked Raina.

Raina shrugged. "You never know with Berry," she said.

Berry appeared with a piece of fruit leather and spread it over the cone's wide opening. "Okay," she said. "Melli, now try and talk," she instructed.

This time when Melli spoke, her voice came

through the cone muffled and
distant. She really did sound
like a ghost!

"Berry!" Melli cried.
"You did it! What a great
idea."

"*Ghoul* work," Cocoa told
her, laughing at her own joke.

Berry grinned. "Never hurts to have a little
fruit around," she said.

Dash picked up the telescope. "We'd better
get down to the fields fast," she said. "Those
Chuchies are working quickly."

"So it's okay if we use your shawl?" Melli
asked Berry.

"Yes," Berry said. "Licking lollipops! This
might work!"

The five fairies grabbed the supplies and headed down to the fields. In the dim light they worked to make the ghost stand up and loom over the fields. They pushed the lollipop stick deep into the ground. Then they tied another stick across, making a T shape so the ghost would appear to have two arms.

Melli stood back and admired their ghost.

"The ghost needs eyes," Cocoa whispered. "He has to see what the Chuchies are doing!"

"Hold on," Dash said. "I think I have two more peppermints. A ghost should have glowing eyes, don't you think?" From her pocket Dash took out her last two candies and stuck them onto the shawl. The bright green mints looked like glowing, ghoulish eyes.

"Hot caramel!" Melli said very quietly. "I think we've got a ghost! Let's move this ghost closer to the Chuchies."

Now all they had to do was convince the Chuchies that there was a ghost haunting Candy Corn Fields.

Ghost Lessons

Together, the five fairies were flying down to the north side of Candy Corn Fields. Each of them held on to the lollipop stick that formed the body of the ghost. They zoomed quickly through the air, heading down to begin their plan to save Caramel Moon.

"Now this really looks real," Dash said. She

glanced over her shoulder. "Doesn't this look like a flying ghost?"

"Shhh," Cocoa shushed her. "We don't want the Chuchies to hear us. We have to set up first." She pointed to the bunch of Chuchies gathering up the candy corn. They were so focused on their task that they didn't even look up.

"Oh, I hope this works," Melli whispered. She kept her eyes focused on the fields below. Her heart ached as she noticed all the dirt mounds that the Chuchies had made by digging tunnels.

What a gooey mess, she thought.

"Everything is going to be okay," Cocoa said. She knew from Melli's expression that she was worried. "We'll get the Chuchies out of here and still save the crops in time for Caramel Moon."

More than anything, Melli wanted to believe her best friend. But she wasn't one hundred percent sure the plan would work. Chuchies were known to be mischievous, but would they scare so easily? Would they listen?

The friends landed on the soft brown sugar ground. They huddled behind a lush green stalk and found a good spot for the ghost.

"On the count of three," Cocoa said, "let's lift the ghost up and stick it into the ground."

"One, two, three," Berry counted.

The fairies heaved the ghost up and secured the stick in the ground.

Standing back, Berry grinned. "Sure as sugar, this looks like a spooky ghost to me!" she said in a hushed voice.

"Let's hide over here," Raina suggested. She

pointed behind a stalk. "We'll be able to see, but we'll be well hidden. Melli, do you have the sugar cone?"

"I do," Melli said. She took the cone from her bag. Then she took a deep breath. "Here I go...." She held the cone with the end wrapped in fruit leather. In her loudest, deepest voice, she called, "Who is there?"

Peeking out from their hiding places, the fairies watched the Chuchies freeze.

"Meee, meee, meee?" a Chuchie sang out, shaking.

A few Chuchies put down their baskets and turned around. They seemed panicked. And then they noticed the ghost.

"Who is stealing my candy?" Melli said

into the cone. She peeked around the stalk to see what the Chuchies were doing.

"Keep talking," Raina whispered. "You've got their attention!"

"I am the Ghost of Candy Corn Fields," Melli said. "These candies are for the Caramel Moon Festival."

A few more Chuchies gathered around. All the hairs on their pom-pom bodies were standing up straight!

They are listening, Melli thought. *The plan is working!*

"You are not allowed to take this candy!" Melli continued. "The candy here is for sharing, not for stealing."

"Meeeeeeeeeeee!" a chorus of Chuchies cried.

Dash put her hand to her mouth to quiet

her giggles. She couldn't believe the Chuchies believed their lollipop ghost was real.

Cocoa gave her a stern look, reminding her to be serious.

Raina squeezed Dash's hand. And the four of them kept careful watch.

"They're leaving!" Raina whispered. "Look!"

Melli put down the cone and saw that Raina was right. The Chuchies were crawling back into their tunnels.

"Let's keep the ghost up here in the field," Raina suggested, "just to be sure that the Chuchies don't come back."

"I don't think they're coming back," Berry said as she watched the furry little creatures scurry back into their holes.

"Maybe Mogu didn't put them up to this?"

Cocoa asked. The Chuchies lived in the Black Licorice Swamp, where only pretzels grew along the banks of the dark, salty shores. The Chuchies craved sweet treats and often tried to get Candy Fairy candy.

"If Mogu was behind all this, he won't be pleased," Raina said. "But from what I've read about Chuchies, they won't be back here. They were definitely spooked."

"Sure as sugar," Melli said with a grin. She hugged her friends. "We got the Chuchies to leave!" She fluttered her wings and flew up in the air.

"I had no doubt," Berry said, folding her arms across her chest.

Before Cocoa could respond, Melli flew back down to her friends.

"The fields look terrible!" Melli cried. "The tunnels the Chuchies dug have ruined the ground."

Dash shot up in the air and checked out the area. "Wow, those Chuchies sure were fast."

"And messy," Raina said, joining Dash in the air. "They only ate the top parts of the candy corn and left the yellow-and-orange parts on the ground." She shook her head. "We need a clean-up plan."

"And soon," Berry added. She shot up in the air next to her friends. "Caramel Moon is tomorrow night!"

Melli knew her friends were right. Scaring the Chuchies away was only the beginning. There was more work to be done to prepare for the festival.

Gazing up at the lollipop ghost, Melli was thankful the Chuchies were gone. "Good job," she said. "Thank you, Ghost of Candy Corn Fields."

Berry smiled. "Wearing my new shawl, it's definitely the best-dressed ghost," she said, laughing.

"Don't worry, Berry," Melli told her. "I'll make sure to get this back to you before Caramel Moon."

Thinking of Caramel Moon made Melli a little nervous. Could she and her friends get the fields cleaned up before the full moon?

8

Clean-up Crew

The first light of morning peeked through the clouds high above the Frosted Mountains. Melli squinted up at the rising sun.

"Come on," she called to her friends. "We must finish cleaning up the fields before daylight."

Even though she was tired, Melli kept on

working. She reached for a few pieces of candy corn on the ground and put them in her basket. She had already collected a mound of half-eaten candy corn, but there were still yellow-and-orange pieces of candy scattered.

Since the Chuchies had left the fields, she and her friends had been picking up all the half-eaten candies. Still, the fields were a mess. The mounds of dirt from the Chuchies' tunnels made Candy Corn Fields a difficult maze to manage. Normally, all the fairies danced around the stalks as they picked the candy. And this year with the Sugar Pops playing, there'd be more dancing than ever before.

Where will everyone dance? Melli wondered.

She thought back to when her sister had told her about the Sugar Pops coming to the festival.

She had been so excited and had imagined dancing all night under the Caramel Moon. Now those thoughts were buried—there'd be no dancing tonight. The Sugar Pops would probably not want to come.

Then a terribly sour thought popped into her head.

What if the festival is canceled?

"Ready?" Cocoa asked, grabbing a handle of the basket. She looked over at Melli.

When Melli didn't answer, Cocoa snapped her fingers in front of her friend's face. "Melli!" she said. "Are you listening?"

Cocoa's voice brought Melli out of her thoughts.

"Sorry," she said. "I'm ready now."

Melli threw two more pieces into the overflowing basket. Then she lifted up her end of the basket and flapped her wings with all her might. The basket was heavy. "Those Chuchies took more of the crops than I had thought," Melli said, sighing. "And they wasted so many of the candies. Look at all these half-eaten pieces!"

The two fairies flew to the edge of the field and dumped the basket.

Melli wiped her hand on her forehead. "I'm not sure those stalks on the north side are ready to harvest," she said to Cocoa. "The tunnels dug up part of the crops there. I'm afraid this prank that the Chuchies played is going to affect the festival."

"You worry too much," Berry said, flying up behind her. "I think we all need to rest."

Raina and Dash dumped their basket of

ruined candy corn onto the pile. "We've been working all night," Raina added.

"Rest?" Melli cried. "How can I rest? Look at this field."

Cocoa took out a piece of chocolate bark from her bag. "Everyone calm down," she said. "Let's take a break and think about our next move."

"You have any more chocolate bark?" Dash asked, licking her lips. She was always hungry, and seeing Cocoa with that chocolate made her even hungrier. Dash might have been tiny, but her appetite wasn't! "I think better on a full stomach," she added.

"Here you go, Dash." Cocoa smiled as she handed Dash a piece of chocolate. When Cocoa offered a piece to Melli, she shook her head. She wasn't hungry. "What am I going to tell Princess

Lolli?" she asked. Even though the gentle fairy ruled over Candy Kingdom with a sweet and truthful touch, Melli was nervous. She didn't want to disappoint her.

"Tell me what?" a sweet voice asked.

The five fairies looked up and saw the beautiful fairy princess hovering above them.

"Good morning," Princess Lolli said as she flew down beside the fairies. Her strawberry-blond hair fell loosely around her shoulders, and her candy-jeweled crown sparkled in the morning light. "You look as if you've been up all night!" she exclaimed.

"We have been," Melli told the ruling princess. She bowed her head. "We've been trying to clean up the mess."

Princess Lolli looked around the fields. "The

Chuchies have been here, haven't they?" she said. "I can spot their messy work. Those creatures are slow to learn." She shook her head. "Their greed always gets them into trouble."

"We taught them a lesson!" Dash blurted out.

Raising her eyebrows, Princess Lolli said, "Tell me what happened."

As Melli told the princess the story of the Chuchies and the Ghost of Candy Corn Fields, Princess Lolli nodded.

"I see," the fairy princess said at the end of Melli's tale. "While scaring someone isn't very nice, teaching them that there are consequences to stealing is an important and valuable lesson."

"But what about Caramel Moon?" Melli asked. Her wings twitched. She was so nervous about what Princess Lolli would say.

"Is it true that the Sugar Pops are coming?" Berry asked.

Princess Lolli grinned. "Yes, the Sugar Pops are coming to play tonight," she told the fairies. "Your clean-up crew has done good work, but I'm afraid we've got lots to do before the festival." She took a small pouch from her bag. "Here is some magic sugar dust," she said. "I think this will help the crops on the north side. After such an invasion, the crops need to feel secure to sweeten fully."

"How can we help?" Melli asked. "We want to make sure that the festival happens this year. And that all the Candy Fairies can enjoy the candy corn."

"There is something that you can do," Princess Lolli said. Her silver wings fluttered. "Are you willing?"

Melli and her friends all nodded. They were eager to do whatever the fairy princess told them. The thought of not having a Caramel Moon Festival was too bitter to consider.

9

Sugar Dust

Do you really think this will work?" Melli asked Raina. While the others were still collecting the ruined candies, Melli pulled Raina aside. "Have you ever read anything about this magic sugar dust that Princess Lolli gave us?"

"I haven't," Raina admitted. She shook her head slowly. She wished she could have told

Melli a story about a time when sugar dust saved a candy corn crop, but she knew of no such tale.

Melli's wings drooped. "Oh." She sighed sadly.

"Remember all those stories about Lupa," Raina told her. "You have to keep up hope. Lupa always saved the day."

"But I'm not Lupa," Melli said, bowing her head. She turned and saw the ghost still standing in the fields. In the morning light the ghost didn't look as real. The moonlight had helped to create a spooky glow.

"You taught the Chuchies a lesson," Raina reminded her. "You were very clever, and I'm sure the ghost will protect the fields."

The fairies all gathered around Melli. They didn't like to see her so sad.

Cocoa was the first to speak. "Princess Lolli

gave you a task," she said, trying to snap her friend out of her sour state.

Knowing that Cocoa was right, Melli looked down at the pouch of sugar dust.

"Anything Princess Lolli gives is touched with some kind of magic," Raina said kindly. "The first thing you must do is sprinkle the crops."

Melli knew she was right. She hugged her friends and flew to the north side of the fields. Carefully, she spread the fine sugar dust over the crops below. She hoped the sugar dust worked quickly—there wasn't much time!

Just as Princess Lolli had instructed, she tried to think only good thoughts as she threw the fine sugar. She imagined all the fairies in the kingdom picking candy corn, and the sweet smells that would fill the air. She pushed any sour thoughts out of her head and started to hum "Yum Pop." Thinking of her favorite band sweetened her thoughts and made her smile.

When Melli had finished her task, she went back to the spy tower. Her friends had started to take it down.

"We should build another one of these," Dash said. She untied a licorice vine, and two lollipops fell down. "This was fun."

"No thanks," Berry said. "I was freezing all night. I much prefer to sleep inside."

Cocoa saw that Melli was back. "How'd it go?" she asked.

"I did what Princess Lolli told me to do," Melli said to her friends. "I kept thinking of all the fun we'd have tonight."

"Choc-o-rific!" Cocoa exclaimed. "If that's what

you were thinking, then the crops will be extra sweet."

"That's for sure," Berry added. "We're going to have a great time tonight. Especially when the Sugar Pops play!" She touched her hand to her colorful fruit-chew clips. "I made some new fruit jewels for the occasion. I want to sparkle so the Sugar Pops notice me."

Dash rolled her eyes. "I don't think they care about fruit jewels," she told her. "They are very focused on their music."

"It says in *Sugar Beats* that the band loves to entertain," Raina said. All her friends looked at her with wide eyes. "What?" she said. "I read *Sugar Beats* too! There's lots of good information in that magazine."

For the first time since Melli had seen the

Chuchies in the fields, she laughed. It felt good to joke around and be with her friends.

"There's one more thing that Princess Lolli told us to do," Melli said. "Are you all ready?"

The four fairies stood in front of Melli, nodding. "We're ready," they all said together.

They flew down to the edge of the fields to the north side, where the stalks were sunk into the ground.

"Okay," Melli said. "On the count of three, we'll give these stalks a pull."

"Remember to think sweet thoughts!" Raina reminded them.

A cool breeze moved their wings, but the fairies didn't budge from their spots. With their eyes shut tight, each one thought of a sweet memory as she pulled a green stalk up. Each of their thoughts included a time when the friends were all together, and soon the stalks reached their full height.

Melli felt a tingling in her wings and opened her eyes. "I think we might have done it," she said. "At least, I hope so."

"There are a few more stalks to pull," Cocoa said. "We better hurry."

The fairies worked to pull the stalks up, and they kept thinking only sweet thoughts.

"I guess we won't know how the candy tastes until tonight," Dash said. "But I think the fields look much better than earlier today."

"Sure as sugar," Raina said. "Don't worry, Melli. I truly believe this will be one of the best Caramel Moon Festivals ever."

Melli wished with all her heart that her friends

were right. She hoped that Princess Lolli's sugar dust and her friends' sweet thoughts were strong enough to heal the fields. She wouldn't know for sure until that night, when the Caramel Moon rose high in the sky. . . . And she couldn't wait!

CHAPTER 10

Under the Caramel Moon

Melli sat at the top of a caramel tree with Cocoa. As they waited for the first stars of the evening sky to appear, Melli bit her nails. She was so nervous!

"I can't believe tonight is Caramel Moon," Cocoa said. She was swinging her legs back and forth. "I'm so excited to see the Sugar Pops—and eat all that candy corn."

"I know," Melli said. "I've been looking forward to this for so long." She looked down at her bitten nails. "But then the whole Chuchies thing happened."

"But we solved that problem," Cocoa said. "With a little *spooktacular* show."

Melli laughed. "We did, didn't we?" she said. "Let's just hope the crops will be ready by midnight."

"You worry too much," Cocoa told her. "Come on, let's get going. I want a good spot. It's not every day that we get to hear the Sugar Pops!"

"You mean *see* the Sugar Pops!" Melli said, correcting her. "Do you think Char will be wearing his sprinkle hat? I'll just melt if he is!"

They flew over Caramel Hills toward Candy Corn Fields, and Melli held her breath as the moon came into view. The large moon looked like a golden caramel circle in the sky. Seeing the round, full moon rise made Melli fly faster. She couldn't wait to get to the fields. The crisp air sent a shiver down her wings, and she breathed in the sweet scent of ripe candy corn.

"Melli!" Cara called. "Wait up!" The little fairy flew up to her big sister. "I have never seen such a beautiful moonrise. And look at all those fairies!" She pointed down below to the large crowd of fairies flocking to the field. Word that the Sugar Pops were playing had spread far and wide. "Melli, thank you for getting me permission to come."

"You bet," Melli said. She gave her little sister

a hug. Princess Lolli had said it was her pleasure to give Cara permission—especially after all the work Melli had done to save the crops.

"Melli! Cocoa!"

Raina and Dash were waving at their friends. They were standing in front of the stage set up on the north side of the fields.

"We got here early," Raina said as her friends landed beside her.

"But so did everyone else!" Dash added.

Melli looked around. The stalks had returned to their normal height, and there seemed to be plenty of candy corn on the stems. "Everything looks great," she said, amazed.

"They don't call Princess Lolli the ruling fairy princess for nothing," Cocoa chimed in. "I told you that you worry too much."

Melli reached down and plucked a ripe candy corn. She took a bite and her wings flapped with excitement. "Hot caramel!" she exclaimed. "This is the most delicious candy corn ever!"

Each of her friends took a bite and smiled.

"We did it!" Dash said. She reached for more of the colorful candy. "These are my favorite–"

Before she could even finish her thought, Cocoa interrupted her. "We know, candy corn is your favorite candy!"

The friends all laughed. Every candy Dash tasted was her favorite candy!

"Hello, fairies!" Berry cried as she swooped down next to her friends. She was wearing a new dress with brightly colored fruit chews in her hair. She looked beautiful.

"I see you're all ready to meet the Sugar Pops," Cocoa said, eyeing her fancy friend.

"Oh, I can't wait!" Berry exclaimed.

"First we need to pick the candy," Melli said. "After all, that is what this night is all about."

Around them, fairies of all kinds were busy collecting candy corn in large baskets. The fairies were working hard in the bright light of the full moon. And having fun.

Just as Melli and Cara were lifting their basket to dump the candy they had picked into a large barrel, Cara froze.

"Sweet sugar!" Cara screamed. Her dark eyes were focused straight ahead. She couldn't say anything—she could only point.

Following Cara's gaze, Melli saw what had made her sister scream. There on the stage were the Sugar Pops! Chip, Char, and Carob were tuning their gummy guitars.

"Carob's wearing his sprinkle hat." Melli sighed. "He is so sweet!"

As the Sugar Pops started to play, more fairies moved closer to the stage. The music filled the night as all the fairies rejoiced.

Melli stood with her friends close to the stage, listening to the Sugar Pops play.

Princess Lolli appeared on the stage. Her bright pink dress glowed in the moonlight. She greeted the crowd of fairies with a huge smile. "Welcome to the Caramel Moon Festival," she said.

There was a huge roar of applause.

"I am so happy to report that this year's crop was saved by Melli and her friends," the princess said. "We had an unfortunate disturbance, but these fairies came to the rescue. We owe them a huge fairy cheer, and our deepest gratitude."

Melli blushed. She hadn't thought that Princess Lolli would thank them in front of everyone—including the Sugar Pops.

She felt Cara's elbow push her side. "Look," Cara said, pointing to the stage. "You have to go up there! You deserve it. You saved the crops!"

Melli grabbed her friends' hands, and all of them flew up onstage.

"Let's hear it for these fairies," Carob sang out. He turned to Melli. "Do you have a special song request?"

Melli was so overwhelmed that she couldn't

speak! Carob was inches away from her—and his chocolate brown eyes were looking directly at her!

"'Yum Pop' is her favorite song," Cocoa said, coming to her rescue.

"We know that one," Carob teased. He strummed the first chord on his bright red gummy guitar.

Sweet sugar! Melli thought as she swayed onstage to her favorite tune. She was thankful for the Ghost of Candy Corn Fields, and her good friends. All around her, fairies were smiling and singing along with the Sugar Pops.

Lupa would be proud, she thought.

This was a night that would be recorded in the Fairy Code Book. The Caramel Moon Festival was always a supersweet time, but this year had been different. She turned to her friends, and together they all sang "Yum Pop" with Chip, Char, and Carob. The moment was as sweet as the candy corn they had picked.

Cool Mint

For Nathan, my sweet

Contents

CHAPTER 1   Cool Ride   341

CHAPTER 2   Frosty Sun Dip   349

CHAPTER 3   Champion Race   359

CHAPTER 4   Sugar Medal Bravery   369

CHAPTER 5   A Sticky Situation   378

CHAPTER 6   Too Fast   390

CHAPTER 7   Magic Mint   399

CHAPTER 8   Race Day   410

CHAPTER 9   A Little Mint   419

CHAPTER 10   So Mint   428

CHAPTER 1

Cool Ride

A cool morning breeze blew through Marshmallow Marsh. Dash, the smallest Mint Fairy in Sugar Valley, was very excited. She had been working on her new sled all year, and now her work was done. Finally the sled was ready to ride. And just in time! Sledding season was about to begin.

Many fairies in Sugar Valley didn't like the cool months as much as Dash. Each season in Sugar Valley had its own special flavors and candies—and Dash loved them all. She was a small fairy with a large appetite!

Dash was happiest during the winter. All the mint candies were grown in the chilly air that swept through Sugar Valley during the wintertime. She enjoyed the refreshing mint scents and the clean white powdered sugar. But for her, the thrill of competing was the sweetest part of the season. She had waited all year for this chance to try out her new sled!

The Marshmallow Run was one of the brightest highlights of the winter for Dash. The sled race was one of the most competitive and challenging races in Sugar Valley. And for the past two years, Dash had won first place. But this year was different. This year Dash wanted to be the fastest fairy in the kingdom—and set a new speed record. No fairy had been able to beat Pep the Mint Fairy's record in years. He had stopped racing now and was one of Princess Lolli's closest advisers. But no one had come close to breaking his record.

Dash had carefully picked the finest candy to make her sled the fastest. While many of her fairy friends had been playing in the fields, she had been hard at work. She was sure that the slick red licorice blades with iced tips and the cool peppermint seat was going to make her new sled ride perfectly. If she was going to break the record this year, she'd need all the help she could get.

Dash looked around. No one else was on the slopes at this early hour. She took a deep breath. The conditions were perfect for her test run. "Here I go," she said.

On her new sled Dash glided down the powdered sugar trail that led into the white marshmallow peaks. It was a tricky and sticky course, but Dash had done the run so many times she knew every turn and dip of the lower part of the Frosted Mountains. She steered her sled easily and sped down the mountain. The iced tips on the sled's blades made all the difference! She was picking up great speed as she neared the bottom of the slope.

When she reached the finish line, she checked her watch. Had she done it? Had she beat the Candy Kingdom record?

"Holy peppermint!" she cried.

Dash couldn't believe how close she was to beating her best time. She had to shave off a few more seconds to break the record, but this was the fastest run she had ever had. Dash grinned. *This year is my year,* she thought happily.

Suddenly a sugar fly landed on her shoulder with a note. Dash recognized the neat handwriting of her friend Raina. Raina was a Gummy Fairy and always followed the rules of the Fairy Code Book. She was a gentle and kind 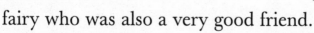 fairy who was also a very good friend.

"Raina told you that you'd find me here, huh?" Dash said to the small fly.

The tiny messenger nodded.

Dash opened Raina's note. "She thinks she has to remind me about Sun Dip," Dash said to the fly. She shook her head, smiling.

Sun Dip was a time when all the fairies came together to talk about their day and share their candy. Dash loved the large feast of the day and enjoyed sharing treats with her friends. Now that the weather was turning colder, her mint candies were all coming up from the ground. Peppermint Grove was sprouting peppermint sticks and mint suckers for the winter season.

Dash looked up and saw the sun was still high above the top of the mountains. She had time for a couple more runs. She was so close to beating the record. How could she stop now?

"Tell Raina that I'll be there as soon as I can," Dash told the sugar fly. The tiny fly nodded. Then he flew off toward Gummy Forest to deliver the message.

Flapping her wings, Dash flew back to the top of the slope with her new sled. She had to keep practicing.

My friends will understand, she thought.

As she reached the top of the slope, Dash could think about only one thing. Wouldn't all the fairies be surprised when the smallest Mint Fairy beat the record? Dash couldn't wait to see their faces! And to get the first-place prize! The sweet success of winning the Marshmallow

Run was a large chocolate marshmallow trophy. It was truly a delicious way to mark the sweet victory of winning the race.

With those happy, sweet thoughts in her head, Dash took off. Cool wind on her face felt great as she picked up speed down the mountain. A few more runs and she'd beat the record, sure as sugar.

This year everyone would be talking about Dash—the fastest Mint Fairy ever!

2

Frosty Sun Dip

Dash flapped her wings quickly, racing toward Red Licorice Lake. She hoped her friends would still be there. She knew that the sun had already dipped below the mountains—and that she was very late. But wait till they heard her great news!

As she neared the sugar beach, Dash saw Raina looking up at the sky. She was pointing toward the Frosted Mountains. "The sun has been down for a long time," she stated. "Soon the stars will be out."

"No sign of Dash?" Melli the Caramel Fairy asked. Squinting, she searched for any sign of her friend.

"Dash has never missed Sun Dip," Cocoa added. The Chocolate Fairy flew up in the sky and scouted the area. "No sign of her."

"Here I am!" Dash called out. Her cheeks were red as she rushed over to her friends. "I know I'm late," she said, starting to explain.

"Let me guess, you were on the slopes?" Berry asked. The Fruit Fairy fluttered her pink wings and settled down on her blanket. "I think all

that time on the other side of Chocolate River is getting to you, Dash. You've never missed a Sun Dip."

"She's all about making the best time for the Marshmallow Run," Melli said, shaking her head.

"She should be concentrating on making the best peppermint sticks instead of a faster sled," Raina mumbled. "Princess Lolli asked Dash to make her two tall peppermint sticks for her new throne in Candy Castle. Did you all know that?" She looked around at her fairy friends. They all looked surprised.

Dash shot Raina a minty glare. "You don't have to talk about me as if I'm not here," she said. "Everything is under control."

The truth was, Dash felt very honored that the ruling fairy princess of Candy Kingdom had asked her to make the sticks for the new throne. When Princess Lolli asked fairies to do something, the fairies all did as she wished. Princess Lolli was a fair and true princess who was very generous and kind. She took good care of the Candy Fairies, and everyone in the valley loved her.

"I don't think Dash has been at Peppermint Grove at all this week," Cocoa said.

"That's not true!" Dash said, flying above her friends. "You don't know the first thing about growing peppermint sticks!"

Melli stepped forward. She didn't like when her friends argued. "Dash, we're just worried about you. It's not like you to miss Sun Dip."

"Or not do as Princess Lolli asks," Cocoa added. "Having peppermint sticks as part of the new throne in Candy Castle is a very big deal."

"That is pretty sweet," Berry said. She turned to Dash. "Have you been working on the peppermint sticks?"

"Yes," Dash said. She landed and planted her feet firmly on the ground.

"How's your new sled?" Melli asked. She sensed that Dash wanted to change the subject— and fast.

"It's *so mint*!" Dash replied with a grin on her face. "I think I have a chance to break Pep's record!" She sat down on Berry's blanket. "How sweet would that be? Today I tied his best time!" Reaching into Berry's basket, she picked a fruit chew and popped it in her mouth.

"Dash!" Berry scolded. "Those chews are not for eating. They're for my necklace that I'm making!" Berry held up a string of sparkled fruit jewels. Berry was very into accessories and never had enough jeweled fruit gems.

"Sorry," Dash said, shrugging. She licked her finger. "It was delicious."

"Did you really tie Pep's record?" Raina asked. "His record has been unbroken for years! No one has even come close to his time."

"Until this year, right, Dash?" Cocoa said.

Dash grinned. "It's all I can think about!"

Raina came over and sat next to Dash on the

blanket. "That's great, Dash," she said. "But you really need to figure out what's going on with your peppermint sticks. Princess Lolli is counting on you."

Melli and Cocoa shared a look. Berry kept her eyes on her fruit-chew necklace.

"You don't understand," Dash said. She looked toward the Frosted Mountains. "This race means everything to me."

"But you have lots of other responsibilities too," Raina said.

"Sorry I missed Sun Dip today," Dash said, getting up. She had just gotten there, but now all she wanted to do was leave. She couldn't stand the look of disappointment on Raina's face.

"Where are you going?" Melli asked.

"Home," Dash said. "I need to frost the tips of the sled again for tomorrow's run."

Raina sank down onto Berry's blanket. "You're not even going to check on the peppermint sticks?"

"I will," Dash assured her friend. "Don't worry."

"But I am worried," Raina said as Dash took off. "I'm very worried."

3

Champion Race

The next morning, Dash flew out to the Frosted Mountains for another early-morning practice. As she flew over Peppermint Grove, she thought about what her friends had said to her. Maybe they were right. She really hadn't been spending as much time as she should have at the grove. She dipped down to see her peppermint sticks.

The strong, fresh, minty smell of the grove greeted Dash as she drew closer. This was a special place for her. She flew by the tiny mint candy bushes. They were budding new delicious-looking minty treats along the edge of the garden. Farther down the grove she spotted the peppermint sticks that were just starting to push out of the sugar soil.

Looking down the row of peppermint sticks, Dash realized that the sticks could have been bigger. She put her hand on one of the sprout sticks.

"This needs more mint," she said. She walked over to a small shed and got her mint can. She knew peppermint sticks needed lots of mint. Since some of these sticks were for Princess Lolli's new throne, she wanted them to be perfect. Even

though her friends thought she didn't care, she did. "I can race *and* raise peppermint sticks," she declared out loud.

While minting the soil, Dash was distracted. She couldn't stay too long in the grove. She had to keep up with her practice schedule. She sighed. If only her friends understood what breaking the Marshmallow Run record meant to her. Maybe then they wouldn't have given her such a hard time at Sun Dip.

Dash poured more white minty liquid into the ground. Then she gently pulled stray mint weeds from around the sticks and straightened the sugar fence around the grove.

There's no need to panic, Dash thought. She stood back and admired the peppermint stick crop.

Maybe she should spend more time here,

she thought, but she had to get going. A cool, refreshing breeze blew her blond hair and tickled her silver wings. She put her mint can back in the shed and headed toward the slopes. Time for another practice run!

Once Dash was on the slope, she double-checked her sled. Everything looked perfect. Just as she was getting ready to take her first run of the day, she sensed someone standing behind her. She turned to see a Mint Fairy. Dash squinted her eyes. And then her jaw dropped.

"Pep?" she said breathlessly. Her heart was beating extra fast.

The Mint Fairy walked over to Dash. "Yes, I'm Pep," he said. "You must be Dash. I've heard a lot about you."

Dash blushed. "You've . . . you've heard

about me?" she stammered. She could barely speak. Standing in front of her was one of the most famous fairies of all time. And certainly the fastest.

Pep laughed. His teeth were as white as the mint syrup Dash had poured around her peppermint sticks. And his bright green eyes twinkled like the sparks from a mint candy.

"Yes, of course I've heard about you," he said, smiling. "You are about to break my speed record, right?"

"I . . . I . . . Well, I hope to break your record," Dash spat out. She looked down at the packed powered sugar by her feet.

Nodding, Pep grinned. "Princess Lolli says you've got a good chance of beating the record," he told her. He winked. "I had to see you take a run for myself."

"I'm about to go now," Dash said.

"Would you like to race me?" Pep asked. He pulled a green mint sled out from behind a tree. "I'm up for a run. Would that be okay?"

All Dash could do was nod her head up and down. She was too excited to say anything! Racing against the most famous speed-racer fairy was a huge thrill. "Sure," Dash finally managed to say. She pulled her snow goggles down over her eyes and got set to race.

"Sweet!" Pep called out. He jumped on his sled and started to count down. "Three, two, one—GO!"

The two Mint Fairies raced down the slope. They were wing to wing for most of the ride, but when the marshmallow turn came, Pep sped ahead, and he won the race.

"Great race!" he said, lifting up his goggles. "Princess Lolli was right about you."

Dash took off her goggles. "Thank you," she said. "I've been practicing. I really want to beat your speed record. But I have big tracks to fill!"

Pep stood up. "You have an excellent chance," he told her. "I wasn't this fast when I was your age. You need to keep up the practicing. Those last turns through the marshmallow are pretty sticky. But with practice, you can do it."

Dash was so happy that Pep understood her wanting to break the record. "It's so great to talk to you," she said. "My friends don't really understand my racing. They keep after me about my candy duties. They don't get my need to race."

"Well, your friends are right too," Pep explained. He pulled his sled off the slope. "It's great to race, but your first responsibility is your candy crops."

"Have you been talking to my friend Raina?" Dash asked, smiling.

Pep shook his head. "No," he said, laughing. "But if she's after you about tending to your chores, then she is a good friend. A real champion is responsible." He wrapped the rope of his sled around his wrist. "Good luck, Dash. I'll be at the Marshmallow Run cheering you on." He flashed her a smile. "Remember, to be a champion, you have to think like a champion." He gave a wave and turned to leave.

"Thanks!" Dash called out. She was still in shock. As she watched Pep fly away, she thought about what he had told her. She squinted up at the sun. She realized a perfect way to make up with her friends. At Sun Dip tonight, she'd bring some special mint candies for her friends . . . along with an apology. A champion apology!

CHAPTER
4

Sugar Medal Bravery

Since Pep had suggested that Dash practice the turns through Marshmallow Marsh, Dash spent the rest of the day on that part of the run, near the bottom of the slope. She weaved in and out of the turns and tried to shave off extra time. If Pep gave her advice, she was going to take it!

With time for one more full run, Dash was feeling confident. She climbed to the top of the slope for her final run of the day.

This time I can beat Pep's record, she thought. *I can be a champion! I know I can.*

She sat for a minute at the starting line and imagined crossing the finish line below in record time. She closed her eyes and took a deep breath.

Think like a champion! she told herself.

She knew this slope. She could break the old record!

With great sped, Dash went down the mountain. She cleared all the turns and jumps in good time. As she neared the Marshmallow Marsh, she steadied herself. She made a sharp left turn and then a quick right. Then she came around a turn, and something was in her way—something that was not supposed to be in the marsh. Dash steered her sled off the slope to avoid a crash and went straight into a sugar mound on the side of the trail.

"Who's there?" a voice grumbled loudly. "Who's that?"

Dash was startled from her near collision. She tried to catch her breath as she took off her goggles. Then she rubbed her eyes. Was she seeing clearly?

"Holy peppermint," she mumbled.

Standing in front of her was Mogu, the salty old troll from Black Licorice Swamp!

"Who are you?" Mogu growled. He stepped forward and stuck his huge nose down in Dash's face. He sniffed around her. "And what do we have here?" The troll peered down at the tasty sled made of the finest candy.

Dash had to think fast! She knew all about Mogu, who loved candy and stole Candy Fairy treats. He was a sour troll who was full of greed. When Mogu had tried to steal Cocoa's chocolate eggs, her friend had been very brave and strong. Cocoa had even gone to the Black Licorice Swamp on the other side of the Frosted Mountains to get the eggs back! Dash knew she had to be brave as well as clever to get out of this sticky situation. No way was that hungry troll going to get her sled as a snack!

"What do you want?" Dash asked, trying to be

strong. She stood up with her hands on her hips.

"Bah-haaaaaaa!" the troll laughed. "Such a tiny fairy. What are you doing here?"

Trying not to get fired up, Dash did her best to be calm. "The question is, what are *you* doing here," she said. "Marshmallow Marsh is far from Black Licorice Swamp."

Mogu sat down on a fallen tree stump, his big belly spilling over his short pants. He stuck his finger into a soft white mound of marshmallow. "I'm double-dipping today," he said, smirking. "I do love marshmallow." He licked his large thumb. Then he eyed Dash carefully. "But your sled looks very tasty too."

"My sled is not for eating!" Dash snapped.

Mogu laughed even louder. He stood up and waddled over to Dash. His white hair stuck out in a ring around his head. "Oh, I'm not sure about that," he said, licking his lips.

The last thing Dash wanted to do right before the Marshmallow Run was to hand over her new sled to Mogu.

Wrinkling his large nose, Mogu laughed again. "I don't really like mint, but I do enjoy licorice and sugar candies. And I see that is what your sled is made of." He leaned closer to the sled. "And frosted tips. Yum!"

Dash backed away. Mogu's stinky breath was awful!

"Let's make this easy," Mogu said, rubbing his big belly. "You just fly away and leave this for me to nibble on. A marshmallow-dipped sled!" He drummed his fingers on his large belly, and a wide grin appeared on his face.

"This is a very sweet surprise to find here in the marsh."

Staring up at Mogu, Dash couldn't help but notice that many of his teeth were missing. And the ones he had were rotten and black. The troll probably never brushed his teeth.

Dash shivered at the idea of the troll eating her hard work. She didn't want to hand over her sled. But what was she to do? Mogu was much bigger than she was, and much stronger. She looked down at her beautiful, fast sled. She couldn't stand the thought of the sled being a snack for Mogu.

Quickly, Dash tried to think of how Raina would advise her. Maybe she would tell her an encouraging story from the Fairy Code Book? And what about Berry, Cocoa, and Melli? They wouldn't be pushed around by a mean troll. After all, Cocoa even faced Mogu under the Black Licorice Bridge!

The time for sugar medal bravery is definitely now, Dash thought. But she was frozen with fear. The closer Mogu came to her, the more scared she became. What was she going to do? How could she save herself and her sled from Mogu?

5

A Sticky Situation

Dash knew she was in a very sticky situation. Mogu was growing impatient, and she didn't want to give up her sled to the greedy troll. She could understand his appetite for her sled, but she couldn't let it happen. She had worked too hard on her sled all year to just hand it over to a hungry old troll! Her small silver wings fluttered as she tried to think of a plan.

"You're a Mint Fairy, aren't you?" Mogu said, sniffing around her. A sly grin spread across his face. "You almost smell good enough to eat."

Dash flew straight up in the air. Mogu reached up and grabbed her leg. "Where do you think you're going?" he grumbled. "I'm not letting you out of my sight!" He pulled Dash down and looked her in the eye. "What's a Mint Fairy like you doing in Marshmallow Marsh, anyway?"

"I'm practicing for the Marshmallow Run," Dash said, breaking free of the troll's grasp. "The race is in two weeks."

"Ah, silly fairy races," Mogu said, waving his hand. "A waste of good candy, that's what I say."

Dash didn't expect Mogu to understand about the race. She stood closer to her sled. She didn't like how the troll was eyeing her prized possession.

"Candy is pretty sparse this time of year," he went on. "Maybe it's because you Mint Fairies are so small. I saw those tiny peppermint sticks in the grove. Those are yours? The tiny ones? Tiny candies for tiny fairies!" Mogu leaned his head back and hooted a large belly laugh. "Oh, I make myself chuckle," he said happily.

Trying to keep her cool, Dash took a deep breath. Her minty nature made her want to lash out at the mean troll, but she knew that wasn't the answer. Her mint candies were the sweetest in Sugar Valley. She had to keep focused on the task at hand. If she was going to outsmart this troll, she had to be clever and calm. Her only chance was to try to trick Mogu. She looked up to the Frosted Mountains, and suddenly she had an idea.

"You know," Dash said, "the Marshmallow Run is the hardest race in Sugar Valley. Only a few fairies take the challenge." She watched Mogu's reaction.

"Oh, please," Mogu said. He waved his chocolate-stained hand in front of his face. "I slide up and down the Frosted Mountains all the time. What's so hard about that?" He shook his head. "And I don't even use a silly sled," he added.

"Well," Dash said slowly, "how about you and I race?" She looked right into Mogu's dark, beady eyes.

"Me race you?" Mogu spat. "Oh, that's a good one," he bellowed. "*Baaa-haaaaa!!*" He hit his hand on his knee and continued to laugh. "You are no match for me. You're a tiny Mint Fairy."

So far he was taking the bait. Dash hoped that she could get the troll up on the slope. She stepped closer to the troll. "Yes, a race," Dash told him. "Just the two of us. And the winner gets to keep this sled." She stepped away from the sled, showing off all the delicious candy.

Mogu raised his bushy eyebrows.

"You could have this sled to race," Dash continued, and then sadly added, "or to eat."

Mogu tapped his thick finger on his chin. "Why should I race you when I can just eat the sled now?"

"I've been the fastest fairy on this slope for the past two years," Dash stated. "You don't think you can beat me?"

Mogu smiled. "Beat you?" the troll asked. "Why, you silly little fairy, of course I can beat you. I'm much bigger and faster." He gazed up at the trail zigzagging down the mountain. Then he looked over at Dash. "Nothing makes me happier than taking candy from a fairy. This will be fun. Let's race."

"Oh, it will be lots of fun," Dash mumbled.

Dash knew the slope was narrow and curvy. Without a sled the troll would have a hard time sliding down. But greed made Mogu answer quickly, and soon they were both up at the starting line.

"Are you ready?" Dash asked, looking over at the troll.

"Let's get this going already," Mogu spat out. "I'm hungry, and that sled of yours is looking delicious." He licked his lips as he looked at Dash's sled.

Dash cringed at the way Mogu was staring at her and her sled. There was no room for mistakes here. She had to keep steady and cross the finish line first. Everything was depending on this run.

"Three, two, one, GO!" Dash cried. She took a running start and jumped on her sled. As she rounded the first turn, Mogu was right next to her. He was laughing as he slid along on his large bottom.

"Oh, this is fun," he yelped as he slid along. "I can't wait for my snack at the bottom!"

Dash knew that there was a sharp turn up ahead, and that she had to reach that turn before Mogu. If she took the lead there, she'd be in

good shape to win. Mogu didn't realize the trail curved down the mountain. She was sure Mogu never went near the slope. He probably only slid down the open part of the mountain.

With great skill Dash took the turn, and the lead. Down the slope she went, gaining more and more speed. Glancing behind her, she saw Mogu struggling to stay on course.

"Ouch, ouch!" Mogu grunted as he squeezed himself through the narrow turn. "What kind of trail is this?"

Dash didn't bother to answer. She just kept going. Trolls cannot be trusted, and she wasn't about to wait around at the end to gloat about her win. She had to cross the finish line and get away as fast as she could. Trolls can't fly, and that was Dash's only way out. She just had to be far enough ahead of Mogu to be out of his reach.

The finish line was up ahead, and Dash could hear Mogu huffing and puffing behind her. On the final turn Dash picked up more speed and crossed the finish line. She had no idea if that run broke Pep's record or not. All that mattered was that she had beaten Mogu!

She lifted her sled up and waved at Mogu.

"Sorry, Mogu!" she called safely from the air. "You've been beaten by the tiniest fairy in Sugar Valley."

"*Argh!*" Mogu bellowed as he came to the finish line. He stayed on his back and looked up in the sky at Dash. "Salty sours!" he cried. He beat his fist on the ground.

Dash couldn't help but grin as she saw the

large troll lying on his back. She flew quickly back to Peppermint Grove. Now more than ever she had lots to prove. She wanted to break the speed record, but also prove Mogu wrong about her candy. She was about to make the best peppermint sticks Candy Kingdom had ever seen.

CHAPTER

6

Too Fast

The fresh scent of peppermint put a smile on Dash's face. She was so happy to be back in Peppermint Grove, far from Mogu. She still couldn't believe that she had challenged the troll to a race and won. Wait until her friends heard about her latest adventure!

Feeling lucky, Dash shined up her sled blades

with some fresh mint syrup. When her sled sparkled, she took the extra syrup over to the mint bushes at the far end of Peppermint Grove. She poured the white liquid on the branches. She took a deep breath, enjoying the magical moment of creating mint.

The tiny mint buds on the bushes glistened in the afternoon sun. Dash thought about how the crop of tiny mints would soon go to Candy Castle. At the castle fairies from all parts of the kingdom could use the flavoring in their own candies. Chocolate mint, sucking candies, and chewing gum all needed mint. Dash hummed happily as she tended to the her crops.

As she worked, Dash thought about what Mogu had said to her. "Salty old troll," Dash mumbled as she weaved her way through the peppermint sticks. Even though she was small, she could still make the best peppermint sticks in Sugar Valley. "You can be sure as sugar!" she grumbled.

A breeze blew her wings, and Dash noticed the sun getting closer to the top of the Frosted Mountains. She grabbed her bag and filled the sack with some fresh mint treats for her friends. She didn't want to be late for Sun Dip again today.

High above Red Licorice Lake, Dash spotted her friends. She was surprised to see all of them there. Was she late? Berry was never on time for Sun Dip. The Fruit Fairy was always the last one to arrive because she took her sweet time getting ready. Dash wondered what the special occasion was for them all to be there early.

"Hello!" Dash greeted the four fairies. They

were all huddled together and didn't see Dash flying in. "You are not going to believe what happened to me today!"

"Oh, Dash," Melli burst out, racing toward her. "Are you all right?"

"Maybe you want to sit down?" Raina asked.

Berry and Cocoa rushed to her side and spread a blanket on the red sugar sand.

"What's going on?" Dash asked, looking at her friends. "What's with the special treatment?"

The fairies all looked at one another. Raina put a hand on Dash's back. "We've heard about the race with Mogu."

"The sugar flies were all buzzing about the news," Berry told her.

"It must have been awful," Melli said, shuddering.

"Were you scared?" Raina asked.

"Wasn't he salty?" Cocoa added, wrinkling her nose.

Dash was a little disappointed that she didn't get to tell her friends about the race with Mogu herself. Those sugar flies were handy for getting messages to friends, but they could spread a story faster than mint spreads on chocolate.

"I'm fine," Dash said. She flew up fast from the blanket. "In fact, I'm great!"

Melli raised her eyebrows. She pushed Cocoa toward Dash.

"He's a tricky one, that Mogu," Cocoa said slowly. "Tell us what happened. Did he challenge you to a race?"

"No," Dash said. She put her hands on her hips. "Is that what the sugar flies told you?"

The fairies all nodded their heads at the same time.

"Yes," Raina said. "They said that he challenged you, but that you won."

"Well, at least the flies got that part of the story right," Dash said. She sat down on a nearby licorice rock. "He wanted to eat my sled. Can you believe that? I had to think fast and come up with a way to get away from him. Challenging him to a race was the only way."

"And the best way," Berry said with a smile. "You outsmarted Mogu! Well done, Dash."

"He said some mean things about mint candies and Mint Fairies," Dash reported. She looked down at her feet.

"He's just a bitter troll," Raina explained. "You shouldn't let his sour words get to you."

"That's right," Berry said. "He's just grumpy."

"Maybe if he didn't go around stealing candy and being so mean, he'd be happier," Melli added.

"Maybe," Dash said. She stood up. "But I want to prove him wrong. The peppermint sticks are going to be extra-tall this year. Princess Lolli wanted a special throne, and she's going to get a supercool minty one!"

"But what about the Marshmallow Run?" Cocoa asked.

"Oh, I can do that too," Dash said. "I have everything under control."

"We've heard that before," Raina said. She had a concerned look on her face. "We could help tend to the peppermint sticks or help you train for the race." She came up beside Dash and put her arm around her friend.

"I can do it," Dash told her. "I might be small, but I can handle this."

"No one said anything about you being small," Berry pointed out. "You just have a lot going on, and we want to help."

"You told me that I wasn't paying attention to my candy," Dash said. "And now I am. I thought you'd be happy." She picked up her bag. "I have to get back to the grove and then do some wing stretches. I have to be in the best shape possible if I am going to break that speed record." And with a wave, Dash was off.

Her four friends watched as Dash flew back to Peppermint Grove, worried that Dash was moving way too fast—even for a Mint Fairy.

7

Magic Mint

Dash admired the tall and very thick peppermint sticks in Peppermint Grove. She grinned as she squinted up at the beautiful, strong candy. For two weeks Dash had carefully cared for the sticks. Early every morning she would arrive at Peppermint Grove and add more mint to the sugar soil. Her magic touch was working, and the sticks were growing beautifully.

Dash had also kept up with her practice schedule for the big race. In the afternoons she did her workouts and runs down the slope. Sticking to her training program was very important. Dash was one busy Mint Fairy.

Fluttering her silver wings, Dash flew over to the mint bushes along the edge of Peppermint Grove. She checked on the tiny white buds on the thin branches. The mints were ready to pick and send over to Candy Castle. Dash sighed. The Marshmallow Run was tomorrow. She really wanted to get two more practice runs in before Sun Dip today. Once the sun went down, she wouldn't be able to take her run down the slope. She'd have to pick the mints tomorrow. Hopefully as a new speed champion!

"Hello, Dash," a cheery voice called out.

Dash watched as Princess Lolli flew over to her. The beautiful fairy princess was wearing her candy-jeweled tiara and a bright pink dress. Her wings glistened in the winter sun as she settled down on the ground.

"I haven't seen you around this past week," the fairy princess said. She flashed Dash a sweet smile.

"I've been here," Dash explained, "and on the Frosted Mountain slope."

"Ah, yes," the princess said. Her strawberry-blond hair bounced around her shoulders. "Are you ready for the race?"

"Yes," Dash said. "I am."

"I heard about your run-in with Mogu," Princess Lolli said. She stared into Dash's blue eyes. "You were very brave. And your fast thinking to challenge him to a race was very smart."

"I had no choice," Dash told her. "I didn't want that salty troll to eat my sled!"

Princess Lolli laughed. "Well, your quick thinking is a match for your speed on the slope. Well done, Dash."

Dash blushed. She was happy that Princess Lolli had come by to see her. She flapped her wings excitedly. "I'd like to show you how the peppermints for your throne are growing," she said proudly.

Princess Lolli flew beside Dash and saw the tall sticks at the far end of the grove. "Dash, these are wonderful!" she exclaimed. "You have been working hard." She touched the beautiful candies

striped with red and white. "These will make my new throne extra-special. Thank you."

"I'm glad," Dash responded. "Now if I can only beat Pep's speed record. I want to be the fastest fairy in Sugar Valley!"

"There is more to the race than just speed," the princess said kindly. "Skill and quick thinking are needed to conquer that slope. I have a feeling that you are going to do very well this year, Dash. You've already proved yourself to be a real champion. I am very proud of you."

Dash's wings fluttered again. She felt like sailing high about the grove. It wasn't every day that Princess Lolli came to visit with so many compliments. Before Dash could respond, she saw her friends flying toward her.

"Hello, Princess Lolli," Raina called.

"We thought we'd come and see Dash," Berry told the princess.

As her friends flew down to Peppermint Grove, Dash smiled. She was glad to see them.

"I must get back to the castle," Princess Lolli said to all the fairies. "It was good to see you all," she added. "You are good friends to check on Dash. She's been very busy!"

"Bye!" Dash called after the fairy princess. "Thank you again for coming!"

"Wow." Melli sighed as the fairy princess flew off. "Princess Lolli just came by to see you?"

"She must have wanted to see how they are growing." Berry flew up to look over the crop of sticks. "And she must have been very happy to see these." She flew over to Dash. "The sticks are beautiful, Dash."

Raina put her arm around Dash. "I'm sorry we gave you a hard time," she said. "You really have come through for Princess Lolli."

Dash looked at her sparkly silver shoes. "Thanks, Raina," she said softly.

"And we don't want you to feel like you are doing this alone," Cocoa told her. "We know that the other Mint Fairies are busy with their crops, so we've come to help you." A wide grin spread across her face.

"Really?" Dash asked.

Berry laughed. "Sure as sugar!" she exclaimed. "Just tell us what to do. We're here to help!"

"Well," Dash said, walking down the grove's path, "if you are serious, I'd love some help picking the mint candies off the bushes. The candies are ready to go to Candy Castle, but

I wanted to get another practice run in before Sun Dip."

"Licking lollipops!" Berry shouted. "That's easy. We can do that in no time, right?" She turned to smile at her friends.

"Sure as sugar," they all said together.

With five fairies working, the bushes were picked clean quickly. When the baskets of fresh mints were lined up, Dash looked over the crop. "Wow," she said. "I never would have finished this so fast. Thanks for helping me out."

"Can we watch you take a practice run?" Melli asked. "I know you're superfast, but I'd love to get a little sneak peek."

"You bet!" Dash said. "I'd love for you all to come."

The fairy friends all flew to the slope on

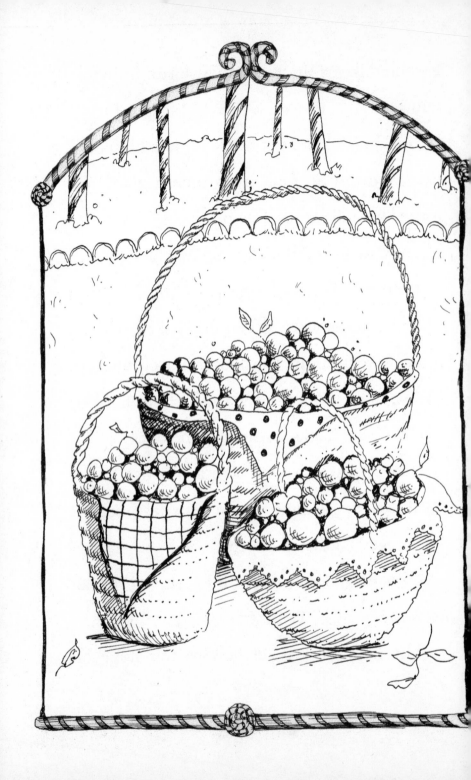

the near side of the Frosted Mountains.

"I'm glad that we don't have to fly *over* the mountain," Cocoa said.

Dash could tell that Cocoa was remembering when she had flown to Black Licorice Swamp to face Mogu. "Hopefully, Mogu will stay on his side of the mountain," Cocoa added.

"I bet he is still embarrassed to have lost the race with Dash," Berry added. She folded her arms over her chest. "Serves him right. He should have known better than to challenge Dash!"

"Now let's see how fast you are," Raina said, smiling at Dash.

Dash picked up her sled and headed for the top of the slope. With her friends by her side, there was nothing she couldn't do!

CHAPTER

8

Race Day

The next morning Dash woke up extra-early. She didn't need an alarm to wake her. Today was race day!

Feeling good, Dash glided over Chocolate River. She took a deep breath. The delicious smell of the river filled the air, and Dash watched the rich brown chocolate rush below her. As much as she wanted to stop and have a quick snack, she kept on flying. She had to get to the Frosted Mountains.

Dash was focused on the race! She had checked on her peppermint sticks earlier that morning, and her candies were perfect. Thanks to her friends, she had gotten all her work done. Now she could concentrate on the race—and breaking the speed record.

When Dash saw the starting line banner, her heart began to beat faster. This was the most thrilling time of all!

Carefully, she iced her sled with fresh mint syrup, making the blades glisten in the morning sun. The cold air rushing around her carried the scent of all the winter candy from Sugar Valley. Dash's tummy rumbled. Again she was tempted to stop her work for a snack. But then she looked at her sled. She wanted to finish her task. Very soon the other racers would be there, and she wanted to be done with her race preparations before they arrived.

"Hey there!" Pep cried as he flew up beside Dash. "You are here nice and early!" He flashed her a toothy grin. "I used to love to get to races early too. Nothing beats the calm before the race, huh?"

Dash nodded. She knew that Pep understood. He held out his hand.

"I brought you some mint candies from my garden," he told her. "I hope you like them."

In Pep's hand were three red-, green-, and white-striped candies. They were beautiful. Dash took one and popped the candy into her

mouth. The candy melted away with a burst of mint in the middle. Her eyes grew wide as she tasted the minty flavor. "Yum!" she exclaimed. "These are extraordinary!"

"Thanks," Pep said shyly. "Now that I am not racing as much, I have more time to tend to my garden." He tossed his long hair out of his eyes. "But I wouldn't have traded all that time racing when I was younger. That was a very happy time for me."

"And for me, too!" Dash said, smiling. "I used to love watching you race. That's why I got into racing."

"Well, you are the favorite today," Pep told her. "And we'll all be cheering for you. Remember, take the course slow around that final bend. The marshmallow gets sticky down there."

Dash nodded. She knew just the area that Pep was talking about. "I will," she said. "And thanks for the candy."

As Pep walked away, Dash saw her friends gathered in tight huddle. They came rushing up to her.

"Lickin' lollipops!" Berry exclaimed. "Was that really Pep? He is even sweeter-looking close up! I've only gotten glimpses of him from the sidelines."

"He is supersweet," Dash said, watching him fly off. "He has been giving me good advice."

Cocoa flapped her wings. "That's nice of him. You could break his record today and he still wants to help you out?"

Dash stood back to admire her polished sled. "Well, he'll always hold that record," she said.

"He's the first ever to have gone that fast. I just hope I can prove myself today."

"I think you've already proved yourself," Raina said kindly. "What Mint Fairy ever challenged Mogu to a race and won?"

"While that fairy was growing candy for a royal throne," Cocoa added.

"And won the Marshmallow Run two years in a row," Melli chimed in.

"Soon to be three years in a row," Berry said, laughing.

Dash smiled at her friends. "Thanks," she said. "It means a lot to me to have you here."

"We'll always be here for you," Raina said. She flew over to Dash and gave her a tight squeeze.

Dash made her way to the starting line. There were more racers than ever before. She looked down the lineup of fairies. There were not only Mint Fairies, but all kinds of fairies from around the kingdom. Dash felt nervous. But then she felt Raina's hand on her arm and saw her friends smiling at her. She placed her goggles over her eyes. She was ready to race!

The caramel horn sounded and the race began! Dash quickly took the lead. She knew the race route well. She held the sled's crossbar tightly and steered down the slope. As she took the turn toward Marshmallow Marsh, she checked behind her. No one was there! She was doing great on time. She hunched down low and tried to gain more speed.

On the next turn Dash felt a bump and then noticed that the left blade on her sled was wobbling. She had no choice but to slow the sled down and pull over to the side. She jumped off to examine the sled. Quickly, she saw the problem.

One of the licorice screws that attached the blade to the sled was missing! Dash looked around on the slope for the sticky peg but couldn't spot it anywhere. How could she continue on? Her sled started to wobble more and more. How could she beat the time—or win—with a broken sled? What was she going to do?

CHAPTER 9

A Little Mint

Dash shook her head. Of all the days for a licorice screw to fall out of her sled! This was the most important race! The Marshmallow Run was only once a year. And this was supposed to be her year to break the record. She kicked the ground with her silver boot. Powdered sugar flew all around. This was not how she thought the race would turn out.

What would Pep do? Dash wondered. As she stared at her sled, she remembered that Pep had skidded off the slope in one race. His sled hit a piece of rock candy. He damaged his sled very badly, and he wasn't able to finish the race.

Dash looked over at her sled and thought again. Riding on a broken sled was very dangerous. Her only chance was to fix the sled. And fast.

I built this sled, she thought. *I can fix it!*

Up on the mountain Dash saw the other racers coming down the slope. She had the lead now, but if she couldn't fix her sled quickly . . .

Dash flapped her wings nervously. The cold mountain air was making her shiver. Down the mountain Dash could see a crowd gathering at the finish line. Pep was waiting for her there—and so were her friends. Knowing that she wasn't alone made her feel stronger and gave her a burst of energy.

She put her hands on her hips. In her side pocket she felt a bottle of mint syrup from her morning's work in Peppermint Grove. Holding up the bottle, she thought about how helpful her friends had been the other day. They had given her a hard time earlier, but in the end they were there for her. Just like this mint!

"Holy peppermint!" Dash cried. "That's the answer!" She smiled. "It's worth a try!" she exclaimed. The bright white liquid seemed to glow in the sunlight. She poured the sticky liquid into the hole and stuck the blade back. "Cool

Mint!" Dash said with a smile on her face. The sticky mint held the blade in place!

"Dash! Are you okay?" Raina asked, suddenly appearing by her side. She turned to the other fairies behind her. "See!" she said. "I knew something was wrong."

"What happened?" Cocoa asked. She flew down and put her hand on Dash's shoulder.

Berry and Melli flew down next to Dash. They all had the same worried expression.

"A licorice screw fell out of my sled," Dash said as she flipped it back over. She looked around at her friends' worried expressions. "But I've solved the problem," she said. "Nothing that a little mint couldn't fix!" She tossed Cocoa the bottle of mint. Then she took a running leap and jumped back on her sled.

"Go, Dash!" Cocoa shouted.

"The others are coming," Melli said nervously.

"Don't worry, you have a good lead," Raina said to Dash. She pointed up the mountain to the other racers. "Go! Go! Go!"

"You can do it, Dash!" Berry cheered. "You can make up the time."

"Thanks," Dash said, looking back at her friends. She was glad they had come by to find her. Hearing their encouraging words made her feel stronger. She could still win and beat Pep's time . . . that is, if she got moving! She looked overhead as her friends flew back to the finish line.

She flapped her wings to gain a little more speed. Up ahead was the stickiest part of the race—the beginning of Marshmallow Marsh.

Taking a deep breath, Dash held on to the bar of the sled. She took the curves quickly, never losing her balance or breaking her speed. She could hear the other racers coming up behind her, but she kept her focus. Up ahead was the finish line. A large crowd of fairies was gathered, and they were cheering loudly.

"Go, Dash!"

"Way to go!"

Dash heard all the cheers, but she didn't look up from the slope. Marshmallow Marsh was gooey, and she had to concentrate. If she veered off the course, she could get stuck in the sticky white marshmallow.

The cheers were getting louder. Dash saw

the rainbow banner of lollipops . . . the finish line! She huddled down low on the sled to pick up speed.

"Dash the Mint Fairy is the first to cross the finish line!" the announcer exclaimed.

There was a roar of applause from the crowd. Dash threw back her head and let out a whoop! In a flash, her friends were around her, giving her a hug. She won!

10

So Mint

"What was my time?" Dash asked. She couldn't see the giant marshmallow clock. There were too many people crowded around her. Her wings were being smushed, and she couldn't fly up to see her official race time. Her heart was beating so fast.

Cocoa took a step back and made room for

Dash to fly up high to see the clock.

Dash's wings drooped, and she sank back down to the ground. "I didn't break the speed record," she reported sadly.

"But you are still the winner of the race!" Raina said, trying to cheer her friend up.

"That's right, Dash," Cocoa said. "You're *so mint*!" She smiled at her friend. "You still came in first!"

Dash nodded, but she still couldn't help but feel disappointed. She had worked so hard to get the fastest time. "Has anyone seen Pep?" she asked her friends. "Maybe he is really disappointed in me," Dash said, looking down at the ground.

"How could he be disappointed in you?" Raina asked. "You were extraordinary out there on the slopes. Many other fairies would have given up or wouldn't have had the strength to finish at all."

"And you didn't just finish," Berry pointed out, "you won!"

"*So mint*," Pep said from behind Berry. He stepped forward with a dazzling smile. "Dash, you made me proud."

"But I didn't break the record," Dash mumbled.

Pep came over to her and put his arm around her. "Not this time, but there's always next year. Plus, it took more skill and bravery to run the race you just did. Remember my race when I skidded off the slope? I didn't have the courage or smarts to do what you did out there today."

Dash felt her cheeks grow redder than the stripes of a peppermint stick!

"I need to thank my friends for making me feel brave," Dash said. She turned to smile at them. "They helped me the most."

"I can see that," Pep said. "You are very lucky."

Before Dash could say another word, Princess Lolli was by her side. "Dash, I heard what happened on the slope. I am very proud of you. You acted wisely and quickly. And you are by far one of the fastest Mint Fairies I have ever seen! Even with your delay, you still came in first. You should be very proud of yourself."

"Thank you," Dash said, bowing her head.

"Come," Princess Lolli said. She held out her hand to Dash. "We are about to have the award ceremony."

Dash took Princess Lolli's hand and flew up to the stage. A crowd of fairies surrounded the stage at the far end of Marshmallow Marsh. A special fruit leather carpet was laid down on the ground for the crowd to stand on and watch.

"I proudly award Dash the Mint Fairy the chocolate marshmallow trophy," Princess Lolli told the crowd.

Flying up to get her award, Dash smiled. Even though she had won two other times, winning this race seemed much sweeter. She proudly took the trophy that was nearly as tall as she was! Then she went back to stand with her friends.

"As many of you know," Princess Lolli continued, "Dash was trying to break the speed record that Pep set a few years ago."

Dash wanted to fly off and hide beneath her wings. She felt everyone in the kingdom staring at her. She was so embarrassed!

"Due to an unexpected problem on the slope today, Dash was not able to break that record," Princess Lolli continued on.

"Why is she telling everyone that?" Dash whispered to Raina.

"Shhh," Raina said. "Let's see what she's going to say."

"What Dash doesn't know is that she broke another record today," Princess Lolli declared. She smiled kindly at the tiny Mint Fairy and waved her back onto the stage. "Dash, no one has ever won three races in a row. You have set a new record!"

Pep squeezed Dash's shoulders from behind. "I never won three races in a row," Pep said. "When my sled sped off the slope, I wasn't able to think as fast and fix my sled. I lost that year."

He gave Dash a little push. "Go up and get your prize. You deserve it."

"And now you'll be listed in the Fairy Code Book!" Raina exclaimed. "All the record holders are in there."

"*Choc-o-rific*, Dash!" Cocoa shouted.

Berry and Melli hugged Dash and then clapped as their friend flew back up to the stage.

"Well done," Princess Lolli told Dash. She handed her a scroll and a beautifully carved piece of wintergreen mint with gold sugar writing. "We're all proud of you."

"Thank you," Dash said. Her feet lifted off the ground as she fluttered her wings happily.

All her friends gathered around her and gave her a hug.

"Come on," Cocoa said, pulling Dash's hand. "Everyone is heading to Peppermint Grove."

"There's more celebrating to be done!" Berry cheered. She twirled around in her new dress and touched her sparkly fruit-chew barrettes. "Dash, you can't miss the peppermint stick presentation."

In the center of Peppermint Grove, Dash had placed her four peppermint sticks for the fairy princess. The sticks were thick and very tall. Perfect for a new throne!

Princess Lolli was thrilled at the size and color of the sticks. "What a perfect treat," she said. "Thank you, Dash. These are the sticks of a true champion. I will always think of that when I sit on my new throne." She reached out to hug Dash.

The rest of the fairies were busy celebrating.

There was music, and there were lots of mint candies around for the fairies to eat. And Cocoa brought a barrel of dark chocolate chips with fresh white sprinkles for everyone. Berry was right—it was a delicious celebration.

Dash plucked a fresh candy cane from the garden. The candy was sweet and refreshing. A smile spread across her face.

Winter was one of the most magical times in Sugar Valley. And winning was definitely sweeter with good friends and some cool mint.

Helen Perelman enjoys candy from all parts of Sugar Valley, but jelly beans, red licorice, and gummy fish are her favorites. She worked in a children's bookstore and was a children's book editor . . . but, sadly, she never worked in a candy store. She now writes full time in New York, where she lives with her husband and two daughters. Visit her online at www.helenperelman.com.